NEW HAVEN FREE PUBLIC LIBRARY
3 5000 09703 1628

No Ordinary Day

No Ordinary Day

Deborah Ellis

GROUNDWOOD BOOKS
HOUSE OF ANANSI PRESS
TORONTO BERKELEY

Published in Canada and the USA in 2011 by Groundwood Books
Fourth printing 2015

Groundwood Books / House of Anansi Press
groundwoodbooks.com

We acknowledge for their financial support of our publishing program the Canada Council for the Arts, the Ontario Arts Council and the Government of Canada.

Canada Council for the Arts
Conseil des Arts du Canada

ONTARIO ARTS COUNCIL
CONSEIL DES ARTS DE L'ONTARIO
an Ontario government agency
un organisme du gouvernement de l'Ontario

With the participation of the Government of Canada
Avec la participation du gouvernement du Canada

Canada

Library and Archives Canada Cataloguing in Publication
Ellis, Deborah
No ordinary day / Deborah Ellis.
ISBN 978-1-55498-134-2 (bound).—ISBN 978-1-55498-108-3 (pbk.)
I. Title.
PS8559.L5494N56 2011 jC813'.54 C2011-900512-3

Cover photograph by Gil Chamberland / Photolibrary
Design by Michael Solomon

Groundwood Books is committed to protecting our natural environment. As part of our efforts, the interior of this book is printed on paper that contains 100% post-consumer recycled fibers, is acid-free and is processed chlorine-free.
Printed and bound in Canada

MIX
Paper from responsible sources
FSC® C004071

Acknowledgments

I WOULD LIKE TO THANK the folks at the Leprosy Mission Hospital in Kolkata, India, for letting me hang out with them and celebrate their work.

To those who are not truly seen

1

The Best Day of My Life

THE BEST DAY OF MY LIFE was the day I found out I was all alone in the world.

This is how it happened.

I was picking up coal.

No. I was supposed to be picking up coal, but I wasn't. I was tired of picking up coal. I was tired of coal.

Being tired of coal in Jharia is no good, because coal is all there is in Jharia. There is coal in pits and coal in piles and coal in mines under the ground. There is coal on the roads and coal in people's hair and coal in people's chests that makes them cough and cough.

There is even coal in the air. It comes up through cracks in the earth from the coal fires that have been burning under the town for nearly one hundred years.

If you're a man, you work in the mines or the pits, hacking at the coal with pickaxes and shovels.

If you're a woman, you walk up the narrow steep trails with large heavy baskets of coal on your head.

If you're a child, you run around and pick up any stray lumps of coal you can find. If the bosses see you doing this they'll chase you, and they'll hit you if they catch you. So you have to move fast.

On this very happy day I was supposed to be picking up coal. I had my coal bag over my shoulder. There was a bit of coal in it but not very much. Instead of running around the coal fields, I was trying to convince the shopkeeper that I had a coin in my hand.

"Let me see it," said Mr. Bannerjee. He sat in his chair and flicked his horsetail fly swatter around.

"Oh, it's right here," I said, holding up my clenched fist.

"What is it? Twenty paisas? Ten? You can buy one sweet, maybe two. Choose, and then pay and go."

I stretched out the moment before I replied. Mr. Bannerjee had a tiny television set in his shop, on a shelf next to the jars of skin-whitening cream. The picture it showed was fizzy, and it jumped up and down, but I could still see the Bollywood dancers. I waved my head the way the dancers did, trying to remember the steps to try later.

"Choose. Then pay and go," he repeated.

Mr. Bannerjee's shop was made of scrap wood and old cardboard boxes, and it was completely open on one side. He slept in it at night to keep thieves away. But he didn't want anyone watching his TV unless they were customers.

"What did you say?"

"You heard what I said!" Mr. Bannerjee waved his fly swatter in bigger circles, but I wasn't worried. He didn't like to leave his chair. It was a bit of a game I played sometimes, seeing how long I could watch his television before he chased me away.

He knew I didn't really have any money. I never had any money.

I managed to stay a few moments longer. Then the TV went to full fizz, and there was no point in hanging around.

I wandered down to the railway tracks, picking up bits of coal when I saw them but not putting any effort into looking.

Piles of trash lined the tracks. Ragpickers and goats poked through it.

I stayed away from the bigger piles of garbage. I didn't feel like getting into an argument, and ragpickers sometimes guarded their territory.

I kept my eyes on my feet and shuffled garbage around with my toes. I wished I was a goat. Goats ate everything. If I was a goat, I would never be hungry.

"Hey, there's Valli. Valli, come and throw rocks with us or we'll throw rocks at you."

I looked up. Some of my cousins were out on the tracks with their friends. None of them liked me. I didn't know why.

"She won't. She's too scared."

That was my cousin Sanjay. He was my size and never forgave me for the time I beat him up when we were younger. I wasn't allowed to eat until he was finished, and then I was given whatever food was left on his plate. He started stuffing himself, just to watch me be hungry. I stood it for three days. Then I let him have it. Smashed the metal plate down on his stupid head. I got a beating from my uncle for it, but Sanjay always left at least some food behind after that.

He got back at me in other ways, though. Sneaky ways. Like kicking me at night so it was hard to go to sleep. He called me names like pig-face and dirt-brain. I tried to insult him back but my words didn't have as much power as his. He knew he was worth more than me. We both knew it.

I was afraid to throw rocks but I couldn't let him see that. And I couldn't let his friends see that I was scared. If they did, they would be on me faster than a goat on garbage.

I walked quickly into the middle of the pack and picked up a rock.

Just looking at the targets made me shake.

On the other side of the tracks, a stone's throw away, monsters lived among the garbage dumps and dung heaps. Their faces were not human. Some had no noses. Some had hands without fingers that they waved in the air as they tried to protect their heads from our rocks.

But I didn't care, as long as they stayed on their side of the tracks. They were unclean, foul creatures. They carried the sins of a former life, and if you got too close, they would turn you into one of them.

That's what my uncle said.

"You eat too much!" he would scream, when the pain in his chest got bad and he had no money for drink to make it better. "I'll break your arms and send you down the tracks to beg with those animals! You are a curse to me!"

And then, in the night, his voice quiet and his breath in my ear, telling me to make no noise or the monsters would grab me in my sleep, drag me away and tear me apart. And I would tremble and bite my lip and pray to the gods for the sun to rise.

I slowly pulled my arm back to get ready for the throw.

I closed my eyes and let my rock fly. I didn't know if it hit one of them or not.

One of the stones came flying back at us.

Sanjay bent down to pick it up.

"Don't touch it! You'll turn into a monster just like them," one of my cousin's friends shouted. "That's one of the ways they get their victims."

Sanjay picked up another rock instead. They were all too busy throwing and laughing to pay attention to me.

I slipped back until I was behind the group.

The boys had dropped their coal bags to free their arms for throwing stones. Their bags had coal in them. Coal that would look better in my bag than it did in theirs.

I crouched down. In an instant I grabbed one of the coal bags and started to run.

I managed to take a few steps before a kid slammed me with a thud into the dirt.

"Thief! Coal thief! Coal thief!"

The others piled on top of me. I swung my arms and kicked and tried to get away. But I couldn't throw off so many kids.

They worked together, pounding me and pulling my hair. They lifted me up. I saw the ground fall away.

"Throw her to the monsters!"

"Let them eat her. That will teach her!"

I screamed. I tried harder to get away from their clutches. I pulled and twisted, but they hung on tight.

They carried me over the railway tracks, getting closer to the monsters with every step.

And then they threw me.

And I landed. Right in the middle of the monsters.

I landed on monster arms and legs and laps and elbows. I was smothered by rags and dirt and bodies.

I could feel them reaching for me, grabbing at me, bumping up against me. I knew they were getting ready to eat me or tear me apart.

I screamed. I breathed in filth and foulness and felt like I was going to throw up.

I could hear the kids laughing on the other side of the tracks. They would stand there and watch me be torn to shreds and devoured, and they would just keep on laughing.

I punched and kicked and twisted until I broke free and rolled away, hitting my head on the track rail. Then I jumped to my feet and ran.

I ran with my eyes full of tears. I stepped in dung and pushed people out of my way, but I didn't care. I bolted across the tracks and screamed as a train whistle blew.

I left the tracks and walked back to the coal fields. I walked until the shakiness left me and I could feel a bit of victory.

I had escaped from the monsters. They hadn't eaten me.

And then I kept walking because I had no place

to go, no place where people wanted me to be with them. I kept on walking because I didn't know what else to do.

Then I heard the bell.

It was a bicycle bell, ringing over and over, getting closer and closer.

Along with the ringing, a man's voice called out.

"School today! Free school! Everyone is welcome at my school! Come to school today!"

Every few days the teacher came to our village. On the back of his bicycle was a box with a school inside it — chalk, maps, school books. A piece of chalkboard was tied across the top of the box. He rode his bike through the village, ringing the bell and gathering children together.

The teacher always set up his school on the empty bit of land behind the tea shop. All my aunt's children were allowed to go except for the baby. There was always a baby. And there was my oldest cousin, Elamma. It was her job to take care of the family.

Elamma did not like me. She couldn't go to school, either.

By the time I got to the tea-house yard, the teacher had set up his chalkboard. He covered the chalkboard with words and numbers. When he ran out of room on the chalkboard, he picked up a piece of coal and wrote on the mud brick wall.

"She's not supposed to be here!" One of my cousins pointed at me. I was leaning into the folds of a banyan tree at the back of the yard, out of the way.

"Education is for everyone," the teacher said, as I knew he would. He continued with the lesson.

The teacher liked me.

I remembered what he taught us and, if I was around when he took his meal break, he gave me extra lessons while he ate his rice and dal.

Once he gave me a notebook and a pencil.

My cousins took them from me soon after, but I had them for a little while.

I formed letters and words in the dirt with a stick. I could read some English and Hindi words on billboards and packages. I knew how to add up money, although I never had money. I knew that the moon traveled around the earth somewhere up there in the deep, dark sky.

I leaned against the banyan tree and watched. And listened. And formed my letters in the dirt and did sums in my head.

That's where Elamma found me on the best day of my life.

She hit me. Hard.

"You're supposed to be working."

The baby on her hip started to cry.

The children in the yard thought we were more

interesting than the lesson the teacher was trying to teach. They left the bit of chalkboard and formed a ring around me and Elamma.

"Fight! Fight! Fight!" they chanted.

"I'll work later," I told Elamma. I couldn't hit her back because she was holding the baby. "The coal is not going anywhere."

"You'll work now. I have to work. Why should you get to go to school when I can't? I'm the oldest! I should get something for that!"

She hit me again, which wasn't fair because, as I've said, I couldn't hit her back.

"You are welcome to come here, too," the teacher said. He was trying to get everyone back to the chalkboard. "Bring the baby."

"And who will do the cooking? Who will do the laundry? You're a man. You think these things happen like magic." Elamma turned her back to the teacher, grabbed me and pulled me away.

The children laughed and pointed.

"If you let her stand here again," Elamma called back to the teacher, "my father will run you out of the village."

I had to laugh at that, even though it made her madder. Her father spent all his time coughing up blood, hitting my aunt and drinking up all the money my aunt made carrying coal.

I knew Elamma wanted to hit me for laughing, but she couldn't hit me without letting go of me, and if she let go of me I was going to bolt. So I got away with laughing at her.

But not for long.

She dragged me through the village. She was strong from so many years of lifting and carrying babies.

"Where is your coal bag?"

I froze. I looked down at my side, hoping the bag would magically appear.

"I dropped it," I whispered.

"Those things cost money. Where did you drop it? And don't tell me you don't know."

"It's with the monsters." I could feel myself start to tremble. "Across the train tracks."

Elamma shifted her hand from my arm to the back of my neck and marched me through the village. I tried to squirm away but she dug her fingers into my skin.

She dragged me to the railway tracks, to the rags and boards and piles of garbage where the monsters with no noses lived.

"Go get it," she said.

"I'm not going back over there."

"Go get it." She pushed me to the ground.

I was free. I could have run, but where would I go?

"If you come home without it, he'll blame me,"

Elamma said. "He'll beat you, but he'll beat me worse. You know he will. So here is your choice. Go and get the coal bag, and come home with it full of coal. Or don't come home at all."

I thought of the stuffy little one-room shack where we all lived and slept. The cookstove smoke made the coal air even thicker. The room had mosquitoes and spiders, flies and ants that no amount of sweeping could get rid of. The whole family slept squished together on the dirt floor. There was hardly ever money for kerosene, so when the sun went down, the nights were long. It was a long way to the community toilet and the little ones often didn't make it.

The shack always smelled bad. Always.

But sometimes we had enough food and we played games like seeing who could stare the longest. My aunt taught us songs about animals. When my uncle was sober and not coughing, he would pretend that the little ones could hit him and make him fall over.

It was home.

I didn't know how Elamma could keep me from going back there without my coal bag. I just knew she would.

I stood up and took a few steps forward to the middle of the tracks. I waited there for a moment, half hoping a train would come and run me over.

"Get moving," Elamma said behind me.

I took a few more steps. I saw the monsters watching me.

And then something happened.

A girl stepped out of the monster pile and came toward me. She looked like me, but shorter. She didn't look like a monster, but I knew she must be one because she lived with them.

She was smiling. And carrying my coal bag.

It was all folded up in a neat and tidy square with sharp edges and pointy corners.

She held it out to me.

I didn't take it. I was afraid to get that close to her.

We stood that way for a long minute. Then the smile left her face. It wilted away like a weed drooping in the dry season.

She put the coal bag on the ground and walked away.

I didn't want to pick it up. I was afraid that I would turn into a monster by touching what a monster had touched.

But I was more afraid of what Elamma would do to me if I didn't pick up the bag. So I picked it up and crossed back over the tracks.

"I was hoping you wouldn't do it," Elamma said. "It would have been nice to get rid of you. More room for the family."

"I'm family, too."

Elamma didn't say anything for a moment.

Then she said, "No. You're not."

"My mother was the sister of your mother," I said. "That makes us family."

"Your mother was a sickly woman who died bringing you into the world," she said. "Your grandparents gave my parents money to take you off their hands. They were neighbors. Even after they got rid of you, they had to move away."

"Why?"

"Your mother shamed her family," Elamma said. "You have no father."

She held her head a little higher when she said these words. Then came her big finish.

"You had better get used to carrying coal. That's all you will ever be good for. You'll never get a husband. And stay away from that school. Knowing how to read won't make you better at carrying coal. Now, get to work."

She let me go and walked away.

I stood alone. After a while I started to pick up bits of coal that had fallen off a cart or out of somebody's basket. I put the coal into my bag. My bag got heavier.

I thought about what Elamma had said.

I had been told my parents were dead. I had never met them, so I didn't think about them.

Now I thought about them.

I decided Elamma was lying. But I had to be sure.

I headed over to the pit where I knew my aunt was working. I sat on the edge of the pit, dangled my feet and waited.

The pit was so big our whole village could be dropped into it and there would still be room left over. Dust rose up from the coal diggers at the bottom and from the feet of the women climbing in and out of the pit. I could hear the sound of pickaxes hitting rock.

The sun was shining but not much light got through the haze of coal dust and the smoke from the coal burning underneath the ground. I saw a few trees, but the leaves were gray, not green. If the sky was blue, it kept it a secret.

Everything was gray.

Except for the line of women coming up the trail from the pit. Their saris were points of bright colors. Not even the haze could blot them out.

It took a lot of scrubbing to get the coal dust out of those saris. I knew. It was one of my jobs to fetch the water to wash my aunt's sari clean.

My own clothes were gray. All I had to wear was what I was wearing. The coal was in them forever. That was just the way it was.

I watched the bright colors moving through the fog of dust. I imagined that the women were birds, strange birds, and that I was sitting on the moon.

Could people really sit on the moon? If they could, it would look a lot like Jharia. I had seen the moon when it was round and big. It looked like dust and coal pits.

I was thinking about this so hard that I almost missed my aunt. Then I saw her, loaded down with a large basket of coal on her head, almost at the top of the path that led from the pit.

I ran over to her.

"Auntie, I need to talk to you."

"Is your coal bag full? It's not even half full."

"I need to ask you a question."

She kept walking. She wanted to dump her load of coal. The bosses were standing by the truck, so I held back. I didn't want them to ask what was in my sack. They might take my coal without paying for it.

My aunt joined the line of ladies waiting by the truck. They dumped their baskets into the back of the truck. Workers on top of the truck shoveled the coal so it wouldn't slide off.

When her basket was empty, she came back to me.

"Talk quickly. The bosses are in a bad mood."

"Elamma said that I'm not really her cousin."

"What? I can't hear you." She bent down so that her face was closer to mine. Her face was lined with coal dust and sweat. Coal dust was even in her teeth.

"She said you're not my mother's sister. She said

my mother was just your neighbor, and that we are not family."

"Child, look where you are standing!"

I was standing on top of one of the cracks that had opened up in the ground. Smoke was climbing up my legs. Hot coals were underneath my feet.

My aunt moved me away and kneeled down to look for burns. I could see a hot piece of coal smoldering red against the bottom of my foot.

"You've gone and hurt yourself," she said. "Now how are you going to work? How are we going to get you medicine?"

I pulled my leg out of her hand.

"Auntie, I'm fine. I don't feel anything. Is it true?"

She looked up at me. "Is what true?"

"Are we really not family?"

She was busy dusting coal and ashes off the bottom of my foot with the hem of her sari. For a moment I thought she wasn't going to answer me.

Then she did.

"We are not family," she said. "Your mother's parents gave us some money to take you in. That's why you live with us."

The bosses started yelling at her to get back to work. She put her hand gently on my shoulder and held it there for a moment. Then she picked up her basket and headed back into the pit for more coal.

I watched her go down the steep pathway until she got so far away that I could no longer pick her out from the other ladies with saris and baskets.

I was looking at my future.

I suppose I had always known it. What else could I ever do? But knowing something was different from admitting it.

On that day, that day for truth, I admitted it.

And when I looked clearly down the years at what I would become, another truth came into my head.

I had no family.

You stayed with your family because they were your family and families were supposed to stick together and care for each other.

But I had no family.

And I had no friends.

I had no reason to stay.

The truck behind me was getting quite full of coal. The worker jumped down from the back. The sides and flap were locked into place. The driver finished talking to the bosses and got behind the wheel. Another man got into the truck beside him. I heard the motor start up.

The bosses had their backs turned.

I was moving before I started to think about it.

I was good at moving fast. I was good at climbing

and I had magic feet that didn't feel the rough points and edges of hard chunks of coal.

In an instant I was at the truck, over the side and crawling to the top of the coal pile. The truck started to move. Coal fell off as I tried to dig myself into the pile. I watched children below scramble to gather it up.

The truck went through my village.

It passed the shack that belonged to the woman who was not my aunt.

Elamma was outside, sweeping the dust out the door. She had to hold the broom with one hand because her other arm was still holding the baby.

She saw me.

She started to call out for the truck to stop. It was moving slowly.

Instead, she dropped her broom. It hit the ground with a bang. She moved quickly toward the truck.

I think she wanted to come with me. She even reached out to try to grab onto the back.

Then she remembered the baby.

Even then, she looked around for a place to put it down.

There wasn't a place. She was stuck.

I watched her cry as the truck rumbled out of the village and out of Jharia.

2

The Moving Mountain

RIDING ON A PILE OF COAL was fun while the truck moved slowly through the village. It got scary as the truck turned onto a highway and picked up speed.

It was scary, but it was also exciting. I had never ridden on anything faster than a hand cart. I had never been away from my village, not once in all my life. All I had ever seen was coal.

Now I saw green. Real green, not green covered by gray. I saw fields and trees and paddies of rice and lakes full of water lilies. The sky was bright blue, the wildflowers were yellow and purple and pink. I saw buffalo and donkeys, mango trees and rows of cauliflower, tea plantations and bamboo stacked high for building.

I didn't know most of the time what I was looking

at. We were moving so fast that I felt like I was a bird, flying high and fast and looking down at the world.

The deeper I buried myself in the coal, the safer I felt. The weight of the coal on my back kept me from slipping off the mountain. Just my face peered out of the pile. I rested my chin on my hands and watched the road roll out behind me.

I didn't think at all. I just looked.

Even after the sun went down, I looked out hard into the night. My eyes grabbed at any bit of light. The moon rose. It was full. I felt like the happiness would just burst right out of me.

The truck stopped a couple of times, pulling off to the side of the highway to refuel and for the driver and his buddy to take a break. I stayed still and quiet and kept my head down. I could smell pakoras and bhaji. My stomach rumbled, but I didn't pay any attention. I had been hungry before.

The truck kept rolling all night long. At some point I fell asleep.

I woke up to daylight and a man crouching down in the coal beside me, shovel in hand and swearing.

"What is this?" he demanded.

I heard another voice.

"Raj! What's the holdup?"

Raj stood up. "We've got a stowaway!"

"What?"

I heard the other man scramble up before I could see him. The way I was buried in the coal did not allow me to raise my head very much, so I only saw the lower parts of their legs. One of them smashed his shovel against the coal right near my face.

"When did this happen?"

"How should I know?"

"Didn't you check?"

"Do I have to do everything?"

Back and forth they yelled at each other.

I don't like shouting. It almost always goes along with hitting. I put my face down in the coal and covered my head with my hands.

"We should call the police," Raj said.

"If we call the police, we'll be stuck here for hours. That's if we're lucky. Maybe they'll think we stole the kid. Maybe they'll arrest us."

"Look, Kam, maybe the child is dead. Buried in coal dust like that, breathing it in."

"Then we have a dead kid to explain. How is that better?"

"We leave the body by the side of the road. Not here. We find a rice paddy or a mangrove swamp. If the kid gets found, no one knows anything."

"We're not that lucky," Kam said. "The kid's alive. Look."

I was wiggling a little, trying to get more of my

arms out of the coal so I could protect m

"We could always kill it," Kam said.

The words hung in the air.

I didn't know what the men were th
was not going to let myself be killed. I had seen some wondrous things on the journey so far. I wanted to see a lot more before I died. I was too small to be much of a fighter against two grown men, but I could throw coal and I could bite and there were probably many other things I could do to make them think twice about killing me.

I could feel coal being tossed off my back. Hands grabbed my shoulders and pulled me out.

I was trembling.

I kept my eyes closed. It was less scary that way. They carried me down from the coal mountain and stood me on my feet beside the truck.

"We could still leave him by the side of the road," Kam, the shorter man, said.

"Would you want someone to do that to your child? What's your name?" Raj asked me. He was taller than Kam and had a scruff of a beard that he rubbed as he talked. "Why were you on our truck? You could have fallen off and been killed. Did someone put you there?"

The questions came too fast for me to answer them.

Then he had another thought.

"Is there anyone else up there? Hey, Kam, grab your shovel. There may be more kids buried up there!"

"There is no one else," I said.

"Wait." He peered closer. They both did. I was so thickly covered in coal dust it was probably hard to see that I was even a person.

"It's a girl."

"My name is Valli."

"Who put you up to this? Your parents trying to get rid of you? What kind of parent would put his child in a truck full of coal?"

"I don't have parents," I said. "It was my own idea."

"Why would you do that?"

"Because ... because I don't like coal."

"She doesn't like coal," Kam said. "She looks like she's taken a bath in it, but she doesn't like it."

"Now we *have* to call the police," Raj said. "We can't leave a little girl by the side of the highway."

The two men started arguing again. I was getting bored, so I left them to it and walked away. I didn't know where I was but that was fine with me. I was somewhere. And I was going somewhere else.

I saw a lot of buildings and a lot of houses and little shops. The road was much busier with cars and trucks than my village road. On one side of the highway was the coal depot, which was not at all interesting, but everything else was new and different.

I hadn't gone far when Kam grabbed my arm.

"Where do you think you're going?"

I pointed up the road.

"It's not that easy." He steered me back to the truck.

They seemed to have reached some sort of decision.

"Here's what's going to happen," Kam said. "You're going to get in the truck and keep quiet. We'll unload the coal and then we'll take you to a woman we know. Her name is Mrs. Mukerjee. She might give you a home."

"That's no life for a little girl," Raj said. "She should be in school."

"What school will take her with no parents and no papers? And will you pay the fees? How many children are you paying for now? Don't worry," Kam said to me. "This will work."

He took me to the front of the truck and opened the door. I needed help to climb in. It was very high up.

The floor of the truck was littered with all kinds of things — empty crisp packets, cigarette butts, bottle caps. I sorted through it, looking for money. I didn't find any. I licked the crumbs out of the crisp packets. They were salty and good.

When the men came back they got into the front seat. I had to stay down at their feet, which I did not like. Their feet were dirty and took up a lot of room. Plus, I couldn't see out the window.

We didn't drive for long before we stopped again. They got out. I smelled food, but I was shocked when they brought me tea and dosas. I ate in the truck. It was food I hadn't worked for, food bought special for me, not left over from the children who were not my cousins.

They got back in the truck and then it was all start and stop, stop and start as the traffic got thick. I could hear the car horns and smell the exhaust. I felt the truck turn this way and that. I heard the driver yell at people who cut across his path, and I heard people yell at him when he got in their way. It was quite funny to hear, but I wished I could see.

And then the truck came to a full stop and the motor was shut off.

"Look, I'm still not sure ..." Raj said.

"Quit fussing," Kam said. "We're here, aren't we? The decision is made. Get up, kid. This is the end of the ride for you."

3

The Butterfly Woman

THEY LIFTED ME OUT of the truck and took me into an alley.

Everything was cement.

No. It wasn't. There were lots of other things.

There was a man sitting in a shop, tapping leather into shoes.

There was a woman pushing a cart full of bad-smelling stuff she had cleaned out of a latrine.

An alcove held a statue of the goddess Kali, all black with her red tongue pointing out. A young man in a suit and tie stood before her, praying.

Above me I heard a baby crying, and someone was playing music.

I couldn't stop grinning.

"There is so much going on," I said. "Thank you for bringing me here!"

"Don't thank us," Raj said.

They banged loudly on a green door. No one answered.

"Are you sure she's in there?"

"She's there. Where else would she be?"

They knocked again. They kept knocking until a middle-aged woman shouted down at them from an open window up above.

"Are you men crazy? You know my girls don't get up until eleven. And I don't rise before noon. Go away."

"Mrs. Mukerjee. We have something for you."

"Anything you have can wait until regular business hours."

She disappeared inside, banging the window shut.

The men knocked again.

The window flapped open.

"You don't want to make me angry," she said.

"Mrs. Mukerjee, look!"

I was made to move away from the door and out into the alley where she could see me.

"What in the world is that?" the woman asked.

"It's a girl."

"I don't believe you."

She started to go back inside.

"She has no parents!"

She stopped and leaned out the window again,

taking a hard look at me. I waved a bit and tried to smile. She made me nervous, but I wanted to make a good impression.

"My name is Valli," I said. "Good morning." I made the namaste, pointing my fingers together and giving a little bow.

"The only good morning is mid-afternoon," she said, lighting up a cheroot. She breathed out a puff of smoke. "I'm coming down."

She disappeared. Then after a moment she opened the green door.

"How do I know you didn't steal her?" she asked. "I have enough trouble with the police."

"I climbed on the back of their coal truck," I said. "They didn't know. I wanted to get away from Jharia."

"Wanted the bright lights of the big city, did you? Looks like you brought Jharia with you." She stared at me some more. "What were you doing in Jharia?"

"Picking up coal," I said. "That's all there is to do. But I can read and write and I can speak a little English." I started to recite the English alphabet, to impress her. I was prepared to go on to Bible verses if necessary. The bicycle teacher had taught us a few of them.

Mrs. Mukerjee waved me to a stop after the letter j. "And where are your parents?"

"Dead," I said, even though I didn't know about

my father. "I was living with my aunt but she turned out not to be my aunt, so I left."

She bent down and stared at me, eyeball to eyeball. "I don't like liars."

I didn't even blink. "Neither do I."

She straightened up and talked to the men. "All right, boys. What do you propose?"

"We thought a finder's fee might be in order," Kam said.

"A fee? You want me to pay you? For taking a runaway off your hands?"

"We should have taken her to the nuns," Raj said. "We should have dropped her off at a temple." He took my hand.

"Not so fast." Kam stopped him. "We brought her to you because we know you'll treat her right. She seems intelligent. She could work for you. And for that, a little thank-you is not out of the question."

"Intelligent?" Mrs. Mukerjee repeated. "I'm not so sure. See how she's looking at me, like I'm from the moon or something. Girl, why are you looking at me like that?"

"You look like a butterfly," I said. "A beautiful butterfly."

She did, too. The robe she was wearing was loose with wide arms like wings, and the colors were bright and swirly. I hadn't seen many butterflies, but now and then one would stray into Jharia, just for a quick visit.

The men snickered. Mrs. Mukerjee's hand went up to smooth her hair. With the other, she patted her robe.

"We could work out some arrangement," she told the men, "but I'm not giving you cash. That's too much like buying a child, and I'm against that."

"How about we take it out in … trade," Kam suggested.

"I could use a bit of that right now," Raj said.

"I told you, my girls aren't up yet," Mrs. Mukerjee said. "And I need to wash this child off first and see what I've got. There may be nothing but more coal under that coal dust. What do you think, girl? Do you want to come work for me?"

"Will I have to carry coal?" I asked.

"Heavens, no. You'll wear nice clothes and lie around all day. Maybe do a few little household chores, but you won't mind doing your share of those, will you?"

"It sounds good," I said. "But just my share."

"Come back later," Mrs. Mukerjee told the men. "I'll let you know then how much trade she's worth. Go. Your big truck is clogging up the alley."

"Thank you," I said to them again as they walked away.

I wanted to watch them drive away so I could wave goodbye, but Mrs. Mukerjee took me inside and closed the door.

"I'm going back to bed," she said. "Human beings were not meant to be awake this early. My goodness, you are filthy. I'm going to stick you on the roof for now. Don't touch anything."

We climbed up the stone steps, higher and higher. I thought of the woman who was not my aunt, making the long climb up out of the coal pit.

I had never been in a building with so many stairs! I smiled and waved at the sleepy women I saw as I looked into the rooms that opened out onto the landing. Some were sitting on mats and drinking tea. I saw children sweeping floors and being fed by their mothers. I smiled and waved. We were climbing stairs too fast for me to know if any of them waved back.

When we got to the rooftop, I had a quick glimpse of the blue, blue sky and of the other buildings. I wanted to rush over to the low stone wall at the edge of the roof and look down. I had never been up so high!

But Mrs. Mukerjee held me back.

"Time enough for playing later. I have to sleep now or I will be cranky when the business opens. And I can't sleep if I'm worrying about you. So you're in here for a little while."

There was a shed on the roof. She opened the door and put me in it. It was empty except for a mat and a pail.

"Pee in the pail if you have to," she said. "I'll send someone up in a minute with some food. I assume you're hungry."

She closed the door on me before I had the chance to tell her I'd had breakfast already. Then I heard a bolt slide into place and lock me in.

I decided I had better eat every chance I got in case I had to make a run for it.

A few moments later, a very sleepy-looking woman slid back the bolt, handed me a tray of food and locked me in again.

The shed wasn't very sturdy. It was made of wood boards that were nailed together this way and that. Sunlight easily got through them. If I needed to, I could probably just push my way out.

But first I would eat. I drank the hot tea. I wolfed down the roti and I ate the dal. I sat back on the mat with my back to the wall to eat the banana while I looked at the blue sky through the spaces between the boards. I had the whole mat to myself and my belly was full.

I found myself thinking about the woman who was not my aunt and about Elamma, who was not my cousin.

They would both be back at work by now, my aunt in the pit and my cousin carrying the baby. If they were lucky, they had gotten a good night's sleep. But that probably didn't happen. The man who was not my uncle coughed all night, and if he didn't cough it was because he was drunk, and if he was drunk it meant the children were hungry, and if the children were hungry they would have cried all night. There would be more room on the floor without me, but less coal money, too.

Today would be hard for them. Tomorrow would be the same.

It wasn't that I missed them, exactly. But I said a prayer to all the gods and goddesses that one day they, too, would be able to sit on a mat they did not have to share and eat a banana that someone else had worked for.

4

Soap

I DIDN'T TRY to escape. I took advantage of the soft mat and stretched out. I fell asleep.

The bolt sliding back woke me up. Mrs. Mukerjee was there, dressed in a sari instead of a robe. Her hair was combed back. She had two younger women with her.

"You're awfully scrawny," she said. "How old are you? Nine? Ten?"

I didn't know. I shrugged.

"Well, let's see what we've got under all that coal."

We went back down the stairs to a little square cement yard. The water tap was there.

"Burn those clothes," Mrs. Mukerjee ordered the young ones.

"I know how to scrub," I said. "I could wash them."

"Burn them," she said again. They were taken away.

At first Mrs. Mukerjee's assistants just poured water over me. It was cold and felt good. Black streams flowed away from my feet.

"This will take a while," Mrs. Mukerjee said. "I think I could use another cup of tea."

She left the other women to it.

With the top layers of dust off me, they started in with the scrub brushes and soap.

I had used soap before. Not often, because it wasn't food, and food came first when there was money. And the soap only got to me after everyone else in the family had used it first. By then it was gray and slimy.

This soap was different. It had a paper wrapping. When the wrapping came off, I smelled all sorts of wonderful flowers and spices. The lather it made was white and frothy like just-poured goat's milk.

I felt like the star of a Bollywood film.

They washed my hair with soap that poured from a bottle. The lather this soap made was so thick it held all of my hair on the top of my head as if it were a basket of coal. The women let me whoosh it around with my hands. I laughed and they laughed.

I sat on a stool while one of them worked out the tangles in my hair with a comb and twisted it into a long braid. The other took a smaller brush to my fingernails.

When she got to my toenails, she gasped and backed away.

"She's hurt. Her feet are all blistered and scarred."

"They're fine," I said. "I don't hurt at all."

"Look. The child is injured. These are burns."

The other woman looked. I tried to tuck my feet under the stool, but they held my ankles.

Mrs. Mukerjee took that moment to return.

"Is there anything left of her now that the coal is gone?"

"She's too thin," one of the assistants said, "but her face is pretty. The customers will like her. Her feet are injured."

Mrs. Mukerjee took a look.

"How did you do this?" she asked me.

"Jharia is on fire," I said. "It's not a problem."

"You are very brave not to cry with such burns and cuts."

I liked her thinking I was brave, but then I remembered that she didn't like liars.

"I'm not being brave," I told her. "I can't feel anything."

"You can't feel anything?" She circled around me, examining my skin. She lifted the braid off my back.

"Look here." Her assistants gathered around. "Her skin has white patches. Here, too." She pointed to another patch on my upper arm. "And here." She pointed to my thigh and my stomach. "Don't you know what that means?"

"It means I'm getting white," I said. "Soon I'll be all white without even buying whitening cream."

"But the patches will be covered up with clothes during the selection," one woman said. "And in the rooms, the lights are low so — "

"Fools!" Mrs. Mukerjee yelled. "Get her out of here!"

"But …"

Mrs. Mukerjee kept yelling. "She is cursed! Unclean! Get rid of her, now! Where are her clothes?"

"I burned them. You told me to."

"Then find some other clothes for her. Out! Get her out!"

Her assistants jumped into action.

Mrs. Mukerjee grabbed the soap and started to scrub herself vigorously. Then she suddenly stopped.

"Is this the soap they washed you with?"

I nodded.

She screeched and threw it to the other side of the courtyard. She threw with such passion that the soap bounced off the wall and hit her smack in the face.

She screeched some more.

I laughed.

She didn't like that.

"Where is the Dettol? I must bathe in disinfectant. Get out!" she yelled at me. "Get out! Those men had better not come back here. Get me the Dettol!"

She ran into the building.

The courtyard had no exit, and, anyway, I certainly wasn't going anywhere until I had some clothes.

I picked up the soap, wrapped it back in the paper and held it low to my side, hoping the women wouldn't notice. They came back out, breathing through scarves that now covered the lower half of their faces. They tossed some clothes at me and stayed well back. I put on the kurta and trousers.

"What did I do wrong?" I asked.

"You have to go quickly," they told me. "She'll fire us if you're not out of here now. We'll lose our jobs."

I had the rewrapped soap in my hand. I picked up the bottle of liquid soap, too, the soap they had used on my hair. I waited to see if they would tell me to drop it.

They didn't.

Instead, they showed me the exit.

In the blink of an eye I was back in the alley, staring at the closed green door.

"If you ever come back here again, I will tell the police to shoot you," Mrs. Mukerjee yelled down from her window. "In fact, I will shoot you myself."

"What did I do?"

"You are cursed. Now get!"

I went.

I walked down the alley and crossed a busy street.

I heard car horns and bicycle bells and people yelling at me to get out of the way. I knew there were things happening all around me. People passed and bumped against me. Handcarts and animals tried to share the alley.

But I kept my head down. I was too shocked to look around.

I didn't understand what had just happened. Why was she so mad at me? My skin was just my skin. It had nothing to do with how hard I could work or how well I could tell the truth.

A lot had happened in a short time. I was in a strange place. I didn't know anyone, and no one knew me.

I didn't know what to do.

I almost missed the family that wasn't my family. I almost missed the coal.

At least in Jharia, I knew what I was doing.

At least there, I had some place to go.

I walked for a little while from one alley to the other. Then I stopped and sat down on a doorstep. I put the soap on the ground and put my head in my hands.

I closed my eyes. I hoped that when I opened them again I would be back in the world I knew, even if I hated it. I cried.

Life passed by me in the alley. I could hear people, motors, bicycle bells, cart wheels. What did any of it have to do with me? I was invisible. I was nothing in Jharia, and now I was nothing in this strange new place I was in, whatever it was.

"'The burden of sorrow is lightened when I laugh at myself.'"

Whoever was speaking those words spoke them close to me, but I knew he could not be talking to me. Why would anyone talk to me? I was cursed.

I kept my head down.

"Not a fan of poetry?"

I raised my head.

In front of me was an old man with a long white beard. He wore a torn T-shirt over his thin chest and a red and blue lungi. He was leading a goat along by a rope.

The goat saw my head go up and came to say hello.

The goats in Jharia never said hello to me. They were too busy looking for food. This goat came right up to greet me.

It butted its head against my hands. Its nose was soft. Its mouth was smiling and its eyes looked kind.

The old man smiled.

"See? There are still things to be happy about."

The goat let me scratch the top of its head. When I stopped, it butted my hand until I started scratching again.

"What is poetry?" I asked.

The old man sat down beside me in the doorway.

There was plenty of room. He thought for a moment.

"Poetry is life," he finally said. "Poetry tells us who we are, where we have been and where we are going. It is even more than that. Poetry tells us what we can be."

"I already know what I can be," I said. "Nothing. I'm nothing. I come from nothing, and I have nothing and I'll always be nothing."

"You have soap," the old man pointed out. "Two kinds of soap."

"That's all I have in this world," I told him. "I don't even have any family."

"You have a lovely green kurta," he pointed out. "You have a beautiful long braid down the middle of your back. To someone without clothes and without hair, you are a millionaire."

"The people who gave me this kurta and this braid threw me out. They didn't like the way I look."

"You have a tongue," he said. "And it knows how to form words. You have two hands and two feet and two eyes that can take in all the beauty of my pet goat. To someone who cannot speak, who cannot walk or touch or see ..."

"I'm a millionaire," I finished for him. "But I don't know what to do. I ran away from the place I thought was my home. I have no place to stay, no one to look after me. I don't even know where I am."

"You are lucky," the old man said. "You are on an adventure."

"I'm scared."

"If you were not scared, you would be having just an ordinary day."

That got through to me. I knew what an ordinary day was like. I did not want to go back to that.

Then it was like I could see a picture of myself, sitting on the stoop with my two kinds of soap, petting a goat. It was a pretty funny picture.

I started to laugh. The old man laughed with me.

"Can I stay with you?" I asked. He seemed like a kind man.

"Of course," he said. "You are welcome to the same sky as Margaret and me, the same ground, and the same air. It's yours. Take as much as you want."

I understood. He didn't live anywhere.

"Why do you call your goat Margaret?" I asked. "That's not an Indian name."

"Because when she tilts her head in just the right way, she looks like the former prime minister of England," he chuckled. "Now, you will have to excuse us. We are heading to a particularly promising pile of garbage. Margaret has the great gift of being able to find treasures among the trash."

He got up to go.

"But what should I do?" I asked him. I didn't want to start crying again.

He looked at me for a moment.

"Give your soap away," he said.

"Give it away? It's all I have!" Although as I said those words, I knew they were not true.

"Find someone who needs it more than you." He and Margaret walked away.

"Wait!" I got off the stoop and went after him. "I don't know where I am."

He turned around. "Do you remember the poem? 'The burden of my sorrow is lightened when I laugh at myself.' It was written by Rabindranath Tagore. This is his city."

He moved closer to me.

"You have not landed here by accident. This is the city of great artists and thinkers, of writers and dreamers, of mathematicians and scientists. In this city, people have done amazing things. What should you do? You should do something great, like the others who have made this city their home."

He walked away.

I called after him. "But what is the name of this place?"

"My child, you are in the city of the gods. You are in Kolkata."

As he said the name, the skies opened up. Water poured down from the heavens.

The rainy season had begun.

All around me, people scurried to get out of the rain.

I let it stream down on me. It ran over my face and down my arms. It flowed over my head like a blessing.

I laughed and laughed.

I felt truly free.

I took the old man's advice.

I found a family living on the street. They had their bits of belongings piled around them — a few cloths, a pot, two cups. The mother and father were soaked to the skin, but their children were dry. The parents held up a sheet of plastic to shelter the little ones. The children sat under it, protected from the rain.

As I walked up to them, the rain stopped as suddenly as it had begun. The sun came out. The streets came alive. Peddlers pulled sheets of plastic away from the fruit, padlocks and pots they were selling. Shoemakers relit the flames under their pots of glue and started tapping away at their heels. Street dogs shook the rain out of their fur and sniffed around. People folded up their umbrellas and kept on rushing.

"Namaste," I said, pointing my hands together as best I could when they were full of soap.

The family did the same, even the youngest.

I held out the bottle of soap and the soap that was wrapped in paper.

At first they shook their heads. They didn't understand. They smiled and spoke in a language I didn't know.

I kept holding out the soap. Finally, they took it. They were happy. They showed the soap to their children. The children sniffed the flowers and spices. Smiles spread across their faces.

I made the namaste again and walked away. It felt good to make the family happy and give them something they needed.

But what now? I wondered.

I felt a hand on my elbow.

The woman was there. She gently pulled me back to the family.

They wanted to share their evening meal with me.

It wasn't much. A bit of dal and a bit of roti. The mother broke the roti and shared it out. We dipped it into the small pot of dal. We couldn't talk to each other, but when the meal was over, they shared songs from their land and I shared a Bollywood song I had seen on the shop owner's TV.

When night came, they made room for me on their bit of pavement.

I slept between two of the children. During the night, one of the toddlers climbed up on my back. I was glad to be a softer mat than the pavement.

In the morning, I left.

Nobody really owns anything. We give back our bodies at the end of our lives. We own our thoughts, but everything else is just borrowed. We use it for a while, then pass it on.

Everything.

We borrow the sun that shines on us today from the people on the other side of the world while they borrow the moon from us. Then we give it back. We can't keep the sun, no matter how afraid we are of the dark.

We borrow our food. What we eat becomes fertilizer that goes back into the earth and gets turned back into food.

Everything is borrowed.

Once I realized that, I stopped worrying about how I would survive.

I didn't need to have anything. I just needed to borrow.

Somehow, that seemed a whole lot easier.

So that became my job. To borrow what I needed. Then to pass it on to someone who needed it more.

It worked. Days turned into weeks and weeks turned into months. I ate. I slept. I lived.

5

Dead Englishmen

SOMEONE WAS BEATING UP Santa Claus.

I was trying to sleep down the street from the Chinese restaurant where the Santa statue usually stood, but the crash of the plastic Santa on the sidewalk woke me up.

Two young men were laughing and talking loudly in English as they kicked the statue between them like a football. From my spot on the pavement I saw Santa's white beard and red cap rise and fall as he was bashed by shoes and sidewalk.

The stray cat that was sleeping beside me to keep warm was startled and got ready to spring. I stroked its fur, trying to get it to stay with me a little longer. But it was too spooked, and it ran off into the night.

Park Street was usually quiet late at night after the restaurants closed up and the tourists went back to their hotels. The men beating up Santa were probably tourists. They were not street people. Street people would not be so rude as to make so much noise and wake up the rest of us.

I hoped they finished their game soon. It was better to stay put at night instead of wandering around. It was too easy to step on something or someone in the dark streets.

But then I heard the police sirens getting closer, and I decided not to hang around.

The police didn't usually bother me. I had been in Kolkata for a few months and I knew how to be invisible. Most people didn't see me. I could stand right in front of tourists and ask for money or food and even they didn't see me.

I wasn't worried about the police coming after me, but the other pavement-sleepers could be a problem. They were waking up all around me.

Kolkata nights could be cold in December. I was afraid they would notice the warm blanket I had. I had borrowed it from the unlocked cupboard at the Metropole Hotel. They had warm blankets at that hotel. I had borrowed from there a few times, although usually from the laundry room before the blankets were folded and put away.

I had on a red jacket, too, with a hood that kept my head warm. I had borrowed it from a pile of old clothes in the market when the stall owner wasn't looking. I felt cozy and comfortable and wanted to stay that way.

I planned to pass the blanket on to someone else in the morning, but there was still a lot of night to get through. I didn't want anyone to borrow it from me before I was finished with it.

I got up and moved away from the storefront where I had been sleeping. It was a store where foreign tourists went to sit at computers and breathe in cold air. During the day it could be a good spot to get money. If you kept your eyes and ears open, you could learn things, like how to sing bits of English songs that played on the radio. If I sang and danced a bit before I asked for money, they were more likely to give.

Or if I told a bit of poetry.

Kolkata has books. Lots of books. Some of them get torn and thrown away. I kept my eyes open and found part of a book that had poems in it — poems that were easy enough for me to read and learn.

I memorized bits of the easiest ones. I didn't need to learn a lot. No one expected much from a girl like me. I could say, "Oh, to be in England, now that spring is here," and tourists thought I was a genius.

I picked up bits of other languages, too. In German I could say "Guten Tag," which means good day. In Japanese I could say "Sayonara," which means goodbye.

Tourists were easy to impress.

The phrase that made them really part with their money was "Welcome to Kolkata. Please give me money so I can go back to school."

A lot of tourists gave me rupees just for that. I spent their rupees on food.

I had tried to go to school. I tried a few different ones.

I would follow the girls in as they got out of their rickshaws and walked past the guard into the yard where they were playing with ropes and balls, their uniforms blue and white or red and white or green and white.

The first time, the guard stopped me at the gate.

The second time, I went in with a group when the guard was busy. I got into the schoolyard. A teacher threw me out.

The third time, I got in through the gate, walked straight through the yard and into an empty classroom.

It was beautiful. Clean and bright and colorful, with a whole piece of chalkboard on the wall and rows of small tables with chairs. I sat down in one of those chairs, pretending that I belonged, trying to be invisible.

I was not invisible to the girl who owned the table. She came into the classroom and squealed and stamped her feet. She said I stank and, as the guard was dragging me away, cried that her chair was now dirty and where would she sit?

But I didn't tell any of that to the tourists. They were busy. They hardly stopped walking even when they were handing out rupees. They had no time for long stories.

During the day the computer store was a good place, but on this night it wasn't.

I wrapped my blanket around my shoulders, stayed close to the shadowy place along the wall of shops and moved quickly away from the sounds of the sirens. I hitched the blanket up so it wouldn't drag along the ground and gather dirt. I wanted it to be in good condition when I passed it along to someone else.

More police came into the street. They zoomed by me, lights flashing. Behind me I could hear the tourists yelling at the police and the police yelling back.

I hated the sound of yelling. Everybody should just be quiet.

I wanted to be off the street, in a place that was soft and dark and didn't smell too bad.

The Park Street Cemetery was the perfect spot, if I could get in. It was always guarded. Lots of dead

Englishmen were buried there. They didn't let just anybody sleep on their graves.

But it was close. If I couldn't get in there, the Lower Circular Road Cemetery was just across the way. And if for some reason that was no good, there was always the Sealdah Railway Station.

By now I knew all the good spots in Kolkata. I had survived the rainy season, when the streets filled with water, and I would survive the winter. Jharia was a long time ago and very far away.

The cemetery guard was asleep.

He was sitting in his chair, inside his little booth just outside the closed gate. I couldn't understand how he could sleep through all the police and all the yelling. Then I got closer and smelled desi-daru, the home-brewed booze that was sold illegally in back alleys. I stayed away from it. The man who was not my uncle had taught me all I needed to know about that stuff.

The guard would have a headache in the morning, I thought. My uncle always had headaches the morning after he drank. He would lie on his mat and hold his head and hit out at anyone who made a noise.

After a quick look around to be sure no one was watching, I flung my Metropole Hotel blanket over the gate. Then I climbed over after it.

The graveyard was calm and dark. The high stone

walls blotted out the sounds of the police and the men they were arresting.

I looked for a soft place to sleep.

I stepped around the other sleepers and went farther along the pathway. I found a good spot behind a big tomb. I was hot now from moving around, so I took off my jacket and rolled it into a ball to make a soft place for my head. Then I wrapped myself up in the blanket and stretched out on the grass. And I spent the rest of the night sleeping among the dead Englishmen.

❋

THE GUARD WAS IN A BAD MOOD when he came through the graveyard in the morning to wake us all up. It was almost funny. I knew he had a headache. I remembered my uncle's face, and the guard was feeling the same pain. His morning was made worse because his boss was also in a bad mood. His boss yelled at him and he yelled at us.

Lucky for me, I was deep in the cemetery. I heard him yelling before he caught me sleeping. I was able to get to my feet, run to the wall, snag my Metropole Hotel blanket on the barbed wire and use it to pull myself up to the top of the wall before the angry guard got to me.

But I forgot my red jacket and left it behind on

the grave. From the top of the wall it looked like a flower I had dropped in the green grass.

I liked to start each day with a bit of fun. It put me in a good mood. I straddled the top of the wall and waited for him. I could see the rusty barbs from the wire sticking into my feet, but I didn't feel anything.

I sat on the wall, my good blanket safely out of the way, and I watched the guard go from sleeper to sleeper. These were all men who were trying to get one more moment of sleep before they had to face the day.

Not like me. I always liked to face the day. That's why I was up and high and out of the way. That's why they were still on the ground, eyes squished shut, being hit across the back by the guard's long stick.

When he had cleared them all out, he looked around. His chest was heaving. His face was pinched with the pain in his head.

"Are you sure you didn't miss anyone?" I called out. And then I laughed because, as I said, I liked to start each day with a bit of fun.

Men don't like it when little girls laugh at them. He came at me, waving his stick and yelling in some dialect I didn't know. But that didn't matter. I knew what he was saying.

He was saying, "Why are you giving me a hard time on this morning that is already so hard? A filthy street girl like you, daring to make fun of a hard-working man like me? Is this what I left my village for? The more you laugh, the more I will beat you. Then we'll see who's laughing."

He was so mad that he couldn't concentrate on beating me properly, and his stick flopped about, barely touching me. When it did reach me, it hit my foot, and I didn't feel it anyway! That just made me laugh harder.

Then I saw in his face that his frustration was getting bigger than my enjoyment, and that's always my signal to find something else to do. A bit of fun could turn into a bit of meanness if you weren't careful, and that wasn't ever how I wanted to start my day.

I ripped my foot out of the barbed wire and hopped down from the wall.

The secret to jumping down from a high wall to the hard pavement was not to land on your feet. You could break an ankle that way. I had seen it happen. I had also seen people get hit by cars or scooters. Sometimes the driver would get out and apologize and take the person into his car. Sometimes the driver kept on going. If the person they hit couldn't afford a rickshaw to ride to the hospital, their ankle or whatever stayed broken. They walked lopsided from then on, dragging their useless foot behind them like a clot of buffalo dung stuck to their sandal.

So I always tried to roll my body to the side when I fell. The pavement was just as hard when you landed, but there was more of you to soak up the hurt. That spread it around. Then you just got to your feet, brushed yourself off and went about your business.

I jumped from the wall, rolling as I went, and I kept rolling when I hit the sidewalk.

I almost rolled into a fortune teller. His parrot leaped and squawked and tried to fly away. Its feathers were clipped, so it couldn't really go anywhere. Parrots were expensive, even for fortune tellers, who could make a lot of money. I had watched them. I had seen the rupees change hands. All the fortune teller had to do was sit and talk and people gave him money.

I decided that would be a good job for me one day, since I could both sit and talk.

I sat on my haunches and spoke softly to the bird until it was resting on its perch again. It looked like it couldn't wait for the next customer to come by.

"You should be more careful," the fortune teller told me.

"You should have known I would jump from the wall and set yourself up farther away."

"How could I know that?"

"You would know if you were a good fortune teller."

"That's not the way it works," he said. "Let me tell

you how it works. I need to know your date of birth, your astrological sign, the alignment of your planet among the heavens."

"Oh," I said. "I thought the bird just picked a card."

Which set the fortune teller off on a long and cheerful explanation of how the bird worked with intuition and how he worked with science and how the two worked together to tell the most accurate fortunes in all of Kolkata. I didn't listen to most of it, but I enjoyed hearing him talk.

So, because he was enjoying himself, and because my hunger was still sleeping, I sat while he explained. Every now and then, when he seemed to be winding down, I tossed in a comment that would get him all excited again, and so we passed a pleasant hour.

"Why don't you give me a demonstration," I suggested. "Tell me how my life will go, and I'll come back and let you know if you were right."

"Do you have any money? You don't. This is how I earn my dal."

"If you're right, I'll tell everyone," I said. "I'll tell the tourists down on Sudder Street. They will all come to you."

The fortune teller twirled his long hair through his fingers and thought.

"I'll tell you a short fortune," he said. "Do you know your birthday?"

"No."

He sighed and squirmed. Then he did what I knew he would do all along. He brought the parrot down from its little perch. The parrot pecked among some fortune cards spread out on the blanket. It picked one up in its beak.

I reached for it, but the fortune teller beat me to it. He stared at the writing on the little card. He frowned, stared at me, then frowned again.

He started to make me nervous.

"Does it say I will be a big Bollywood star?" I joked.

"Excuse my bird. He is not yet awake," he said. "The card says you will soon have many friends."

"You don't think I can have many friends?"

"I don't think you have any friends," he said. "You spent the night in the English cemetery. If you had friends, would they let you do that?"

He was looking a little too pleased with himself.

I couldn't think of anything to say. And I didn't like the way he was smirking.

When I feel mean I want to act mean.

I swooped down at the parrot and yelled a big "Kaaa!" close to its head. It almost jumped out of its feathers.

The fortune teller reached out to soothe his bird, and when he did, his cloak rose away from his body.

That's when I saw his feet.

He had no toes, and his feet were curled in on each other like claws.

He was one of those monsters.

I jumped up. And I ran. Hard.

I ran to make the panic fall away. I ran so fast that my feet did not feel the pavement. They did not feel the stones or the broken glass or the dog droppings or the cow dung.

They did not feel anything.

6

Talking with the Gods

I RAN AS FAR AS I COULD, leaving the monster behind me, until I couldn't run anymore.

Kolkata had woken up.

I could run two steps, then I had to stop and wait as a bicycle loaded with coconuts crossed in front of me. I ran a few more steps, then had to stop again and go around men and boys from the auto-repair shops who had moved their repair work out into Lower Circular Road. I crawled along with the stream of people until I got past the car repairs and into the next block. I ran again, right into a rickshaw that had stopped to pick up passengers — two large men with formal suit vests over their salwar kameez.

"Give some warning before you stop," I said to the rickshaw puller as I moved past him.

"I'll have the customers wave a big flag just for

you," he replied. He groaned as he got the rickshaw moving. His passengers were a lot fatter than he was.

I kept going.

The streets were full of people going to work. And with people already at work, pushing handcarts, pumping pedals on bicycles loaded down with big reed baskets and walking with huge bales of cotton on their heads.

My hunger had woken up just like the city. A cup of morning tea would be a good start. I knew a tea seller on Vivekananda Road who was sometimes friendly. It was a bit of a walk, but I always had time.

The day was warming up quickly. The Metropole Hotel blanket was getting heavy on my shoulders. It was easy to find a family of pavement dwellers who needed a good blanket. Behind a dumpster, next to the wall outside St. James' Church, a woman was trying to keep her toddlers close by. She was nursing a baby and only had one free arm to keep her other kids in line. I didn't see a man. He was probably off looking for work.

I folded the blanket into a tidy square and put it on the ground in front of the mother. She was almost too busy to notice. The children noticed, though. They reached out and patted the blanket with their tiny hands, then snatched their hands back, as if they weren't sure they should. They giggled, then patted it again.

I moved on.

A bicycle came by pulling a cart piled high with bales of rags. I felt like taking a ride so I hopped on the back. I rode in style all the way to Baithakkhana Bazaar before the bicycle man realized he was pulling more weight than he needed to.

"Off! Off! Off!"

I jumped off, smiled and made the namaste. So he had to make the namaste back, and we parted on good terms.

I walked up a few more streets, through the tight markets under the highway flyover, then finally I hit Vivekananda Road.

The tea seller who was sometimes friendly had a stall just outside a cake shop. I liked seeing the little cakes and sweets, so pretty with their colors and decorations. They looked like flowers or treasures from a jewelry store. If I ever got the chance to taste one, I would feel like queen.

The tea seller had just brewed a fresh pot of tea. The steam rose as he poured it from one pot to the other, mixing the milk and tea and sugar.

I could almost taste the hot tea going down my throat. It would give me a warm happy start to the day. I wouldn't feel so hungry with a bit of tea in me.

I stood right beside the tea stall, ready to ask for a blessing, when I hit the first bit of bad luck for the day.

The tea seller's older brother arrived in a rickshaw.

The brother owned the tea stall. He was always in a bad mood.

The brother saw me and started yelling at the tea seller.

"Look how these urchins approach you! Totally without fear. No wonder I am not making enough money. You give away all my profits. You are a thief! Show me you are not a thief, or I will take this stall away from you. I don't care if you are my brother."

The tea seller looked at me. I knew he was about to yell at me even though he didn't want to.

I shrugged a tiny shrug to let him know that it was okay, so he started to yell at me to get away and never come back. Then, in a way his brother couldn't see, he gave me a bit of a hand movement that told me, "Go and wait nearby. This bullock of a brother is leaving soon."

So I backed away and went to sit in a nearby doorway. I watched the metal workers hammer and solder long pieces of metal into railings and bed frames and kept an eye on the older brother, who was waving his arms around and spewing out all sorts of angry words.

Finally the brother called over the rickshaw puller who had been waiting patiently (and who certainly wouldn't get paid for all the time he had wasted waiting). He got back into the seat and the rickshaw puller heaved the rickshaw into a run. They disappeared among the cars and carts.

I went back over to the tea seller's stall.

"I can't give you any tea," he said in a sad way, not mean. "I have to account for all the cups. The number of cups and the money in the box must balance. My brother will check."

That seemed like a small problem.

The cups were small and made of clay. When someone was finished drinking, they threw their cup to the ground. Someone else had the job of going through the streets and collecting the broken cups so they could be taken back to the potter. The potter turned them back into clay, then back into cups again. There were dozens of broken cups lying around on the ground.

I found a cup that was not broken, picked it up out of the gutter and presented it to the tea seller.

"Your brother does not measure tea, does he?"

"That cup is dirty."

It was. I rubbed it with the sleeve of my kurta, the same one given to me when I first got to the city. The kurta was dirty, too.

"Kolkata dirt," I said, holding the cup out again. "It's on me and in me."

He gave up. A stream of hot tea flowed from the kettle into the cup in my hand.

"Drink it quickly," he said. "My brother could come back."

The tea was too hot, so I took it away and sat among the roots of a banyan tree. The tree had come up through the sidewalk, pushing the slabs of cement to the side as it grew.

I sipped my tea next to the clay statues of two gods that had been left there during the Durga-puja. The statues were crumbling a bit. The fingers on one had turned to dust, and part of the nose on the other had disappeared. Their painted-on clothes had once been bright blue and yellow, but the colors were now hidden under a layer of grime.

Still, the gods were smiling and friendly looking. I sipped my tea, held the cup up to their lips in case they were thirsty and asked them if they had enjoyed the festival.

They didn't say anything, but they kept smiling. I smiled with them, and we sat in the sun and enjoyed our tea.

For a few short moments, I didn't feel lonely.

For a few short moments, I almost had friends.

7

The River

I COULD MAKE THINGS HAPPEN.

Just by staring and concentrating hard, I could sometimes make things and people do what I wanted.

It was not a gift I used very often. Only when I needed to.

After I left the tea seller, I needed to.

I was hungry.

By the middle of the day, the full belly feeling of the tea had worn off. It felt like my luck was taking a holiday.

I went down to the river to try to get it back.

In Kolkata they call it the Hooghly. North of Kolkata it's called the Ganges. South of Kolkata it empties into the Bay of Bengal.

I know this because I saw it on a map in a bookstore before the owner threw me out.

I went down to the river and went into the water. People threw coins into the river to be blessed by Mother Ganges. My plan was to pick up some of those coins and use them to buy something to eat.

I had done it many times. Many.

But today I had no luck. I kept diving and feeling around in the mud. I kept coming up with nothing.

I climbed up on an old cement pier to take a rest. When I don't eat for a long time, I can't move as fast or for as long. I get tired faster.

While I was sitting there, I decided to try to use my powers on a little girl who was also sitting on the pier a short distance from me.

She had been lucky. She had a little pile of coins beside her, and she was playing with them, clinking them together over and over and driving me quite crazy.

"Dirvala, come and eat!" A woman waved to the girl from the steps.

"In a minute," the little girl answered.

"Not in a minute. Come now."

The little girl turned her head, pretending not to hear.

The woman went back to arranging food on a cloth. There were a few other people around helping — an older woman, a man, a few more children. They all looked happy and relaxed.

The bathing ghat was busy. The sun was shining

and the day was a little warmer than recent days had been. The broad stone steps down into the water were full of people having picnics, doing yoga or soaping themselves before diving into the water. Others scooped up mud from the river bed, smeared it on their bodies and let it dry in the sun. A couple getting married were performing a ceremony on shore. People were saying prayers and giving offerings of fruit, flowers and incense. A lot of children were diving for coins.

Turn your head, I silently ordered the little girl. Leave your coins alone and turn away. Just for a moment.

I kept concentrating.

The girl's mother called again for her to hurry up. It was time to eat. The girl kept ignoring her.

Then the girl's granny got into the act. One shout from the old lady, the girl dropped her coins and turned her head.

And I pounced.

I had the coins in my hand and was under the water before the girl knew what had happened.

I swam as far as I could, came up for a quick breath of air, then went back down again.

Above me, I heard shouting and yelling when the girl realized her coins were gone. I stayed below the surface of the water for as long as I could at one time. I spat out a mouthful of river, then popped the coins into my mouth so that my hands would be free to move me through the water.

I moved farther out from the shore and let the current take me away. I left the bathing ghat behind and became part of the river, like the boats and the fish.

By bending low and walking on the riverbed, churning up mud with each step, I made my way downriver to the next ghat.

It was a burning ghat, a place for cremating dead bodies. Smoke rose from the wood that helped the dead people burn. Mourners and religious men brought the ashes down the steps to return the dead ones to the river.

There were no other children in the water here. Maybe they didn't like being so close to death. But coins got tossed from burning ghats as well as bathing ghats. People were always hoping for blessings.

I dove, feeling along the riverbed with my hands. I scooped up handfuls of mud and watched it drip through my fingers. Now and then I found a coin. I rinsed the mud off in the river and popped the coin into my mouth with the others.

After a while there were more coins in my mouth than I could hold. I spat them into my palm and headed to shore.

The current was a bit strong and I had to take it slow, stopping to rest now and then.

The burning ghat was not busy. There were just a few people saying prayers, sending off little paper boats with fruit and flower petals and floating garlands of marigolds in the water.

It was peaceful. I heard the sound of chanted prayers. The walls of the temple held back the city noises.

I was almost at the shore when I spotted a woman standing alone by a smoking pyre. Women didn't often come to this ghat. And she was reading a book.

I knotted my coins into a corner of my kurta so she couldn't see that I already had money. Then I moved in to see what she was reading. If she could afford a book, maybe she could afford to give me a few rupees.

She was reading a Bible. An English Bible.

It was perfect.

I knew a few Bible verses. They were useful when I went begging outside the fancier churches on Sundays.

I kept my eyes on her as I moved closer. I didn't want her to run away.

And then I was right next to her.

"'Jesus wept,'" I said.

She was startled, and she looked up from her reading.

"Yes, he did," she said. "Do you know why?"

It seemed like a foolish question, but as I stood there I realized there were all kinds of reasons someone might cry. Maybe Jesus hit his thumb with a hammer. I had seen carpenters in the street do that, and one of them had cried. Maybe he was lonely. Maybe he was thirsty and the tea seller wouldn't give him any tea. Maybe he was lost in a strange city. Or maybe he had heard a great joke and was laughing so hard he started to cry.

The woman was waiting for an answer.

"He was sad?" I said.

"Do you know what made him sad?"

How would I know that?

"He was hungry?" I suggested. "I cry when I'm hungry." I held out my empty hand, hoping she would take the hint. I hoped I wouldn't have to pretend to cry to get my point across.

She glanced at my hand, then looked into my eyes. That made me feel funny.

I lowered my hand. She went back to her Bible.

"My name is Valli," I said. "Are you reading about Jesus being sad?"

I had a feeling that this woman could be good for quite a few rupees — maybe as many as ten — so I hung in.

"No," she said. "I'm reading something happier."

"Are you happy that your family is dead?"

"This man was not my family," she said. "I don't know who he was."

I let her read in peace for a moment while I thought about that.

"Do you come here every day?" I asked. Maybe she just liked to read the Bible at the burning ghat. People did all sorts of strange things. I knew of a park where people gathered every morning just to laugh.

The woman didn't answer right away. I looked up and saw that she was praying so I let her finish. She seemed like a serious woman who would want others to also be serious.

I meant to stand quietly so she would think I was a good child and worth giving rupees to, but a bee started buzzing around my head.

I waved it away. It returned. I thought it might be going to land on my back, so I spun around to shoo it and I lost my balance a little. I didn't fall over, but I worried that the woman might think I was just a child who was playing around, and not a serious child who could discuss why Jesus was crying a lot better if she had a few dosas in her stomach.

"This man died outside the hospital where I work," she said. "No family claimed him. No one knew him, so I — you're standing in hot coals!"

She took my arm and pulled me away.

In trying to escape the bee, I had stepped into the cremation pit where the unknown man was now coal and ashes, ready for the Ganges.

"There was a bee," I started to say. "I didn't mean to disrespect ..."

The woman dropped to the ground and looked at my feet. I had to lean against her while she lifted up one then the other.

"You're burned. And you're cut."

The old pier had a lot of sharp bits of rusty metal on it. I must have scraped my foot on one of them. There was blood on it.

"It's all right," I said, pulling my foot away. "Tell me more about the happy part of the Bible."

I wanted to get her thoughts away from my feet and onto the number of rupees she would give me.

"Who do you live with?" she asked. "Who looks after you?"

"I look after myself," I said. I was starting to feel uneasy. I was used to people asking me questions when I asked them for money, but this woman acted like she really cared about the answers. She wasn't just asking to make herself feel good.

I had enough money to get some food. I started to walk away.

She came after me and took hold of my arm. I knew what was coming next. She wouldn't be the first person to hit me when I tried to get money from them.

I raised my hand to protect my face from the beating.

The knot in my kurta came loose. The coins I had

collected clattered to the ground, mixing with the sand and mud that covered the old stone steps.

"Just hold on," she said. She didn't let go of my arm while she crouched down and picked up all the coins. I kept squirming and trying to pull away.

"Let me go!" I cried out. "Keep the money. Just let me go!"

I was sure a beating was coming.

She gave all the coins back to me. She had me sit beside her on the step until I was able to calm down.

She touched a white patch of skin near my elbow.

"Do you have any more of these?" she asked.

I didn't answer her. I took some mud from the step and rubbed it over the white patch to make it look more like the rest of my skin.

"Your feet are in bad shape," she said. "Tell me, do you feel the burns and the cuts?"

The last time I said I felt no pain, people screamed at me and threw me out of their house.

"Yes," I said. "My feet hurt. A lot."

She kept looking at me.

I shook my head. I felt as though I was doing something wrong, but I didn't know what.

"I have magic feet," I whispered.

"I'd like you to come with me. My name is Indra," she said. "I'm a doctor and I can fix your feet."

"My feet are fine."

"Do you have a home? Yes or no."

I thought of what the old man said on my first day in Kolkata.

"The earth, the sky, the air," I said.

"Where did you sleep last night?"

"The Englishmen's cemetery. But I wanted to sleep there."

"Then maybe you will come with me because you want to," she said. "You'll get a meal and a checkup, and no one will make you stay if you really want to leave."

She let go of my arm. I was free to run away.

She waved the ghat workers over to us. It was their job to put the bodies in the shallow troughs shaped into the cement platform. They built up the fires with small then big sticks of wood. Then they raked the ashes into a container to be carried to the river.

Dr. Indra took some money out of her purse and gave it to them. I knew she had already paid for the cremation. I had spent enough time around the ghats to know how it worked. People had to pay up front because wood was expensive.

She was giving them extra money. She didn't have to. She just did it.

"Thank you," she told them.

And then she held out her hand for them to shake.

I watched the three men hesitate. No one ever

wanted to touch the burning ghat workers. They handled dead bodies. They were unclean.

But the doctor kept her hand held out. One by one, the men shook her hand.

She turned back to me.

"Well?"

I decided to take a chance.

She smiled and led the way.

We left the river and the troughs of smoking fires. We went out through the pavilion where people were getting oil rubdowns, buying incense and flowers for offerings or being shaved by one of the barbers. We went out into the street that was crowded with tea shops and flower peddlers.

The doctor waved over a taxi. She held the door open for me.

I stopped.

"Children get into taxis with strangers and no one ever sees them again," I said. "I don't want to disappear."

"The hospital is some distance," she said. "Your feet really are not good."

"You ride," I said, backing away. "Tell me where to meet you."

She sent the taxi away.

Then she did something I never would have imagined anyone ever doing for me. Ever.

She took her dupatta off her shoulders. From her

purse she took out a small pair of scissors and cut her scarf in half. She wrapped the halves around my feet. She tied the cloth tight so it wouldn't fall off.

"If you can walk that far, so can I," she said.

8

Beautiful Blood

IT WAS A BIT of a walk.

Dr. Indra did not try to hold onto me or make me walk where she could see me. I tried walking behind her and she just kept going. She didn't even look back to see if I was following her. I could have run away any time.

I decided to walk beside her.

She talked to me about what it was like to be a doctor. She said she had to study very hard for a long time. She said she didn't think she could ever learn everything she needed to know, but now it was all in her brain, ready for whenever she needed it.

"It's what I've always wanted to do," she said. "When I was young, all my friends would spend their spare time at the movies. I spent mine with my biology books and volunteering with a street clinic."

"I've never been to the movies," I said.

"I enjoy them now," Dr. Indra told me. "Now that I am doing what I was meant to do, I can take time for things like movies."

She didn't offer to take me to the movies. That was another point in her favor. When I was living at the railway station, a man took a boy I borrowed with to the movies and I never saw him again.

I decided I would trust her enough to let her take me in a tuk-tuk, as long as I sat on the outside.

Dr. Indra waved her hand, and a tuk-tuk pulled out of traffic and came right over to the curb. She got in beside the driver and I squished in beside her, right against the outside railing. We sped off at first, but soon got caught up in the start-and-stop traffic.

I didn't care. I was enjoying myself.

I had hitched rides on the backs of tuk-tuks before, crouched on the bumper with my face pressed against the dusty metal. Sitting in the front was much more fun.

We hit a patch without traffic and the tuk-tuk took off. I swayed into Dr. Indra as the driver swerved his three wheels to zip between a bus and a truck full of melons. Horns blared at us.

I stood up and started to hang off the side to make faces at the other drivers. Dr. Indra pulled me back in, but she did it in a nice way, so I didn't mind.

We got stopped by some cows right in front of the sometimes friendly tea seller. I leaned over the doctor to yell at him and wave.

He didn't notice me. He was too busy looking miserable because his older brother was back. His brother was counting up the little clay cups and comparing his total to something written on a piece of paper.

I watched the older brother put the paper in his shirt pocket, pick up a stack of the clay cups and wave them in the tea seller's face. He lost his grip and the stack of cups started to teeter. Then, one by one, they fell to the sidewalk and smashed.

By the time the cows had crossed the road and our tuk-tuk was moving again, I was laughing so hard I couldn't even see.

"I'm having a really good day!" I called out to the city.

Not long after that, Dr. Indra told the driver to pull over, and the tuk-tuk came to a stop. I was sorry the ride was over, but I was also curious to see what would come next. After all, I was hungry!

Dr. Indra held out her hand for me to take. It was an invitation, not an order. I could take it or leave it.

I decided to take it.

She held my hand loosely. I could easily slip away if I wanted.

We left the sunny, noisy street and walked into a large room that was open to the city at one end and cool and dark at the other. The thick cement walls kept out a lot of the city noise. I saw plants and trees through the windows. It felt like a calm place.

Rows of chairs held rows of people. Some were in business clothes and talking on cellphones. A teenaged boy was wearing jeans. He had plugs in his ears, and he was tapping his feet. A young woman was reading from a big thick book and making notes on a pad of paper. An old man in a long robe and a turban played finger games with the baby on his lap.

No one looked afraid.

The doctor took me past the rows of chairs and through a door into a little room that was also full of people on chairs. A man behind a desk looked up at Dr. Indra.

"Here on your day off?" he asked her. "You can't stay away from us, can you?"

"I have a new friend," the doctor said. "This is Valli."

"Hello, Valli."

He smiled at me. He seemed friendly, but I had learned that you couldn't always trust smiles. Some smiles were lies. Some smiles were followed by hands grabbing at you and pulling you into an alley.

In a quieter voice, the doctor told him, "I need a quiet room for an examination right away. This is not a girl who will wait."

The man looked through some papers.

"The shoemaker is away today," he said. "Will his workshop do?"

"It will," the doctor said. "Perfect."

"And I'll bet Valli would like something to eat," he said. He smiled at me again. I didn't smile back yet. After all, guessing I was hungry and actually giving me food were two different things.

We left the little room and headed up a flight of stairs. The doctor let me into a strange place filled with leather, tools and shoes. Some of the shoes were only half made.

"Can you wait here for a moment?" Dr. Indra asked. "I have to gather a few things, but they are close by and I'll be right back."

I was in a new and interesting place, so I didn't mind having some time to look around. I was about to tell the doctor to leave the door open, but she did it anyway.

By the time she came back carrying a tray full of mysterious things, I had a shoe on each hand and was on my knees, pretending my hands were my feet.

"I can walk with my hands," I laughed.

She laughed, too, and helped me put the shoes back on the shelf.

"Have you ever been looked at by a doctor before?"

"Mrs. Mukerjee looked at me," I said. "The girls

who work for her don't get out of bed until eleven. She likes to sleep until noon."

"And when was this?"

"The truck drivers took me there when I first got to Kolkata," I said. "They wanted to trade me for something, but I don't think she gave them anything because she threw me out. I got this kurta, though." The colors were faded, and there were stains that wouldn't come out. The cloth was torn and worn through in places, but it was nice and clean from being in the river.

"I'm going to listen to your heart beating," Dr. Indra said.

She took a picture off the tray of a person sliced in half. One half was all bones. The other half was all flesh, like the inside of a chicken but prettier. She showed me where the heart was.

"I look like that under my skin?"

"We all do. This is called a stethoscope." She put the ends of it in her ears. Then she put the round part on my chest. "Your heart is beating well. Would you like to hear?"

She put the stethoscope in my ears and I listened to the sound of my own heart beating. It was so amazing I almost ignored the plate of food that someone carried into the room. Almost.

"Wash your hands first," Dr. Indra said as I reached for the plate.

"I just washed in the river."

"Wash in the sink, too." She placed the food on a high shelf and led me to the sink in the corner of the room. She turned on the tap and handed me the soap.

I was amazed at how much dirt came off me. I thought my hands were clean.

I scrubbed until the doctor was satisfied. Then she handed me the food and I sat back down on the bench. There was channa dal to eat, and samosas and cauliflower curry. I had a few coins on me but probably not enough to pay for such a fancy meal. I decided to eat it all fast so they wouldn't be able to take it away once they found out I couldn't pay.

By the time she took some blood out of my arm, I was so happy to have a full belly that I didn't care about the little bit of hurt when the needle went into my skin. I liked to see the glass tube fill up with my nice red blood.

"We'll look at this through the microscope and see what there is to see," she said.

"What's a microscope?"

"It's a special machine that lets us see things that are very, very small. I'll let you have a look. I think you'll like it. But first we need to bandage your feet."

She spent a lot of time cleaning and putting cream on my feet and wrapping them up. Then she gave me a needle called a tetanus shot, which she said would keep me from getting sick.

"Your feet need a lot more attention but I don't want to do more today than you are comfortable with," she said. "I'm sure we can find you a pair of sandals somewhere. Let's go and look at your blood."

She took me into another room. This one had desks, cabinets and more things I had never seen before. A man sat at a high desk, peering into a strange machine.

"We have a young scientist here who would like to see through a microscope," the doctor told him. "She promises to be very careful." She handed him the tube of my blood.

"I'll show you how to prepare a slide." The man put a drop of my blood on a thin piece of glass and added a drop of something from another bottle. "This will stain it and make it easier to see," he said.

He looked first. Then Dr. Indra looked. Then she showed me where to look and how to turn the dials on the machine until the picture became clear.

What I saw was so beautiful I had to back away.

"That came from *me*? It's so beautiful."

"Our bodies are made up of cells," Dr. Indra said. "A cell is a wonderful thing, and one day, perhaps, I will tell you all about it."

"Tell me now."

"Another day. For now let me have another look at your beautiful blood."

I took one more look myself. Then I slid off the stool and let the doctor take my place.

There were some chairs with armrests nearby. Nobody told me not to sit in them, so I sat.

The doctor looked through the microscope for a while. Then she sat down beside me and made a lot of notes on a piece of paper.

My clothes were still damp and I could smell the river on them. I remembered my coins and I made sure the knot holding them was tight. Although my stomach was full for today, I'd need to eat again the next day.

Finally the doctor stopped writing.

"Do you have somewhere to sleep tonight?" she asked.

"Of course."

"Where?"

I waved my arms. "Kolkata."

"Yes, but where in Kolkata?"

I shrugged. The night was a long time away. Why worry about it when the sun was still shining?

She changed the subject.

"The loss of feeling in your feet is caused by a bacteria in your blood. Another sign is the patch of skin on your arm that has no color. You have something called Hansen's Disease. It is also called leprosy. The leprosy germ goes after your nerves and keeps them from working properly. You didn't do anything wrong to get it. The disease is not a punishment. It's just a germ you breathed in. Most people can breathe in the germ and not get the disease. You're part of the five percent of the population that the germ will grow in. Do you understand?"

"Sure," I said, but I wasn't really listening. My stomach was full and the chair was comfortable.

"There is nothing to be afraid of," she said. "This is a disease that has a cure. We can't repair the damage to the nerves that's already been done. But we can get rid of the bacteria and keep the damage from getting worse. We'll start you right away on the pills, and that will be that. Now, the reason I was asking if you had a place to stay is that your feet need to heal. You have some bad ulcers that could use skin grafts to close them up. For that I'd like to keep you in the hospital here for a while. What do you think of that?"

I was sinking into the chair. My eyes kept closing.

She wants to know where you slept last night, I told myself.

There was a ladies' garden not far from the hospital. I could go there and lie down in the cool green grass. The heat of the day was on. I was falling asleep.

Get up and go to the garden, I told myself. But

the thought of rising from the comfort of the chair was too much. Plus, Dr. Indra was sitting very close to me. Her knees were pressed against mine. To leave, I'd have to climb over her.

Too hard, I thought. Too hard.

I couldn't keep my eyes open. My chin dropped to my chest.

I felt the doctor lift me up in her arms. My head rested against her neck and I felt someone carrying me up some stairs. Her skin smelled of flowers. The soft whisper of her voice was kind.

She put me down some place soft.

By the time my head left her shoulder, I was asleep.

❋

"WAKE UP. It's time to eat."

"Let her sleep."

"If she keeps sleeping now, she'll be up all night and then none of us will sleep."

"New girl, wake up. The supper cart is on its way in."

Voices reached me through my sound sleep.

I took my time waking up. I was sleeping on a soft mat in a place that smelled clean. I was very comfortable.

Then I smelled food, and I would rather eat than sleep. Any day.

I opened my eyes.

I screamed.

Monsters stared down at me. I was surrounded by women with scars and women without noses. A woman with no fingers on her hands was shaking me awake, touching me with those stumps.

I jumped off the bed and pushed my way through the women.

"You're not going to get me!"

"She's afraid," I heard.

"Let her go," someone else said. "She's clearly trouble."

"She's a child!"

I broke through and ran out the door. I ran down the stairs, slamming into people who were on their way up.

"Valli, what's wrong? What is it?"

Dr. Indra had me by the shoulders. I tried to squirm away, but her hands were strong.

"Talk to me."

"This is a place for monsters! They'll eat me! They'll tear me apart!"

"This is a hospital for people who are recovering from illness. Nothing more." Her voice was calm but stern.

"They're all monsters up there!"

"Really, Valli? Do you really believe that?" the doctor asked. "You are a human being with a thinking brain. Do you really believe these people are monsters?"

There was too much going on. I was being spoken to in a way I didn't recognize. I was afraid and at the same time I felt a little foolish.

Someone thought I could think. I didn't know what that meant.

Yes, I did. And it frightened me more than the people with the missing fingers.

Dr. Indra let go of my shoulders. She was leaving it up to me.

After making such a fuss, I didn't see how I could back down. Even though I wanted to.

So I looked straight ahead and walked quickly through the waiting room, out of the hospital and back into the street.

9
The Dead Man

"IS HE DEAD?"

Bharati's wide eyes went from the man on the ticket seller's counter to me.

"Yes," I said. "Dead."

She whimpered a little and took a half-step behind me.

In the weeks since I had run away from the hospital, all the niceness had drained out of me. I was like a kid I didn't even know. I wanted to kick at street dogs, steal from blind beggars and rip things from walls.

And be mean to clingy little girls like Bharati.

I was back living at Sealdah Railway Station, where I had stayed off and on in the months I had been in Kolkata. Many children lived there. It had dark corners for sleeping, people to beg from and bits of food that got dropped to the floor by rushing travelers. The railway station was a good place to borrow. A lot of people moved through it, dropping things and leaving their bags open and their backs turned.

Bharati was little and new to the station. She wasn't used to looking after herself.

When I first saw her, she was with her older brother, who brought her food he had worked for and told her to stay put so he would know where to find her.

But he had taken up with the boy-pack. Little sisters were not welcome there.

Her brother was about the same age as me.

I didn't mind Bharati sticking with me sometimes. She was a polite little girl who believed everything I said. But I didn't want her getting any ideas that she could stay with me forever.

"Who put him up there?" she asked, staring at the man. He was flat on his back on the ticket counter, covered head to toe with a blanket.

I had seen it all over and over. I had spent a lot of time at this train station.

"He put himself up there," I said. "And he covered himself up like that, too."

"Why did he do that?" Bharati asked.

"You're full of questions," I said.

"I want to know."

"Because he knew he was going to die, so he

climbed up there so his body wouldn't get wet when the floor washers came."

The floors got washed in the early hours of the day. Anybody who was not awake got soaked by the cold water. Morning in December in Kolkata was cold enough without that. I always made sure I woke up early.

"Why did he cover his face?"

"He didn't want anyone to look at him after he was dead."

"Why not?"

I was getting bored with the conversation and bored with Bharati.

"Because if you look at a dead man's face, his ghost enters your body. Don't you know anything?" I liked to make things up as I went along. Sometimes I didn't know what was going to come out of my mouth until I said it. It kept me entertained.

I reached into my pocket and took out the little bottle of pink fingernail polish I had borrowed from some lady's handbag while I was hitching a ride on a train, begging from passengers. I was aiming for her coin purse, but the train gave a lurch right at that moment and I had to grab what I could.

I headed over to the dead man.

I knew he wasn't really dead.

It was Mr. Vishwas, and he slept up on the ticket counter every night. During the day he worked at his brother's shirt stand in the market. He had been staying at his brother's house, but his brother's wife didn't like him. I heard all about it. He shared his story with anyone who stood still for more than a moment.

I felt sorry for his brother's wife. Mr. Vishwas was always in a bad mood. Always.

"What are you doing?" Bharati said. She grabbed my arm to hold me back.

I shook her off. I was tired of playing nanny. This would get rid of her.

I hopped up on the ticket counter at the foot end of Mr. Vishwas. The blanket covering his face and body didn't quite reach his toes.

I gave the nail-polish bottle a good shake, unscrewed the brush and started to paint his toes.

It didn't take long. It might have, if I had been careful to stay on the nails and not paint his toes as well, but I was more concerned with being fast.

Job done, I waited a moment so that the polish would dry, then rejoined Bharati.

"Now you have to break the spell," I whispered to her.

"The spell?"

"You have to. You were the one to find him. It's you his spirit will come after unless you break the spell. But if you want him to come and get you while you're sleeping ..."

"What do I have to do?"

"It's very simple. Turn around three times, then face him, clap three times very loud and fast and shout, 'Kaaa!' Can you do that?"

She nodded.

This was going to be fun.

"Go ahead," I said. "I'll be right behind you."

I helped her spin three times and turned her so she was facing Mr. Vishwas. Then I ran and hid behind a post.

She clapped three times and yelled, "Kaaa!" at the top of her lungs.

Mr. Vishwas jumped up so fast he fell off the counter.

Bharati screamed and ran into another part of the train station.

Mr. Vishwas picked himself up off the floor, too stunned to be able to chase after her. Then he noticed his bright pink toes.

I laughed and laughed.

But it was a laugh without any joy behind it. Laughing like that made me feel meaner.

Mr. Vishwas came storming after me. He was angry, but I was fast, and I jumped over the gates and ran to the tracks.

I knew he would not follow me. He was too old to jump gates.

I kept laughing as I ran, until I ran smack into Bharati's brother. He was surrounded by the boy-pack. A dozen skinny boys stood near him trying to look tough, their arms folded over their thin chests and torn clothes. Bharati was clutching her brother around the waist and still crying.

"You made my sister cry," he said.

"Your sister cries easily," I told him. I wanted to hurt him. "So do you."

"I do not."

"I heard you the other night. 'Where's my mama! I want my mama!' For a while, I thought your sister had a sister instead of a brother." I looked around at the boy-pack. "Did you boys know you were hanging out with a crybaby?"

Grown men hate it when girls laugh at them. So do un-grown men. I could see Bharati's brother getting angry. I could also see his friends glance at him and frown. They wouldn't want a crybaby in their gang.

I bolted.

Sealdah Railway Station has lots of ways in and out. I knew the boys could run fast. I had to make the most of my head start.

I made it to the side exit. I jumped down the stairs two at a time and ran out into the parking lot.

The boys kept chasing me so I kept running. I zipped into the market under the highway flyover.

It was very dark in there. The sun was hours from rising. The few bare bulbs that were lit up created shadows that made it harder to see instead of easier.

People were sleeping all over the place. On their carts, by their stalls, on the walkways. I came very close to stepping on a lot of them.

The boy-pack kept coming. I could slip through the maze of narrow pathways and not bother anybody, but they were not so lucky. Plus, they were more interested in getting me than they were in not disturbing the sleepers.

Of course they knocked things over. Of course they stepped on people.

I heard the crashes and the shouts. I stopped running and looked back. There was enough light to let me see angry men hitting boys caught up among the poles and canvas of a banged-up fruit stall.

They couldn't see me. I was tucked into a shadow.

But I could see them. I saw the anger on the men's faces. I heard the cries of the boys. I stood and watched and listened.

Fruit spilled all over the ground. A melon rolled over to me and bumped into my ankles. I picked it up, held it close to my chest and walked away.

Kolkata was quiet. There were no traffic sounds to block the noise of the boys crying and screaming. It stayed in my ears for a long, long time.

I kept walking with that melon all along Bow Bazaar Street to Bidhan Sarani, to the area where all the colleges were. I went to Bookstore Alley, sat on the curb and smashed the melon open on the edge of the sidewalk.

The melon was unripe and bitter. I ate the whole thing anyway. The juice ran down my kurta, making it sticky.

What did it matter? What did anything matter?

I had been given a chance, and I threw it away.

I chomped and swallowed, chomped and swallowed until my stomach was aching and full of bitter melon.

Then I threw up in the gutter.

I didn't feel any better.

10

Pizza

I MOVED TO ANOTHER curb away from where I threw up, and then I just sat.

Generally, I liked being in Book Alley. There were dozens of bookstalls and thousands of books. There were old books in Sanskrit, new books in English, and textbooks in Hindi, German and French. All kinds of people came to buy and browse. I could wander from little group to little group, being invisible and listening to their talk. I couldn't understand most of it but I liked it anyway. It made me feel important just to be around it.

On this early morning, though, Book Alley just made me feel worse.

The clean white bandages Dr. Indra had wound around my feet were now gray and filthy. They hung off my ankles. I smoothed the tape with my hand, trying to make it sticky again, but that made no difference.

I wanted clean bandages again.

But I wanted more than that.

I wanted to be like Dr. Indra.

I wanted to know things and to speak about things so that people would listen to me. I wanted to have a purse with rupees in it — enough rupees that I could pay extra for things if I wanted to, just to be nice. I wanted to be able to wave over a taxi or a tuk-tuk and tell the driver to take me someplace and know that I could pay them when we got there. And I wanted to have so many dupattas that I could cut one in half and give it away without even thinking about it.

It was never going to happen. How could it? I was nothing. I wasn't even a coal-picker anymore.

I tried again to smooth the tape down on the bandage so it would stick. Then I got fed up. I tore at the cloth. I ripped away the dressings. I bunched it all up into a ball and threw it as far as I could.

No sooner had the bandages hit the pavement than a young ragpicker walked by, picked them up and added them to his bag. His rag bag trailed behind him. It was almost longer than he was tall. It got snagged on something. The boy had to bend down to loosen it. Then he slowly continued on his way.

I almost went after him, just to be with someone for a little while.

He wouldn't want me, I told myself. So I let him go.

I jumped off the curb, ran through Book Alley and out onto Bidhan Sarani Street.

Traffic was picking up. I grabbed the bumper of the first truck that came by slowly enough for me to catch it. I swung onto the bumper, crouched down behind a stack of hay bales and held on as the truck sped down the road.

Busybody motorists honked and told the driver I was riding on his truck. He stopped, got out and yelled at me to get off. I yelled back, jumped down, ran through the traffic to the other side of the street and grabbed hold of a passing bus. When that stopped, I hopped on the back of a tuk-tuk, then another truck.

I kept moving. I didn't even look at where I was going.

I rode around for hours.

I rode until I was calm enough to realize how hungry I was.

When that happened, I was on the back of a truck loaded with sugar cane. The truck stopped and I hopped off.

Across the street was the New Bengal Shopping Mall. It was big and fancy with bright signs on the high walls and pots of flowers leading up to the entrance. If I could get in, I would be able to get something to eat. The garbage cans there were always full.

But to get in, I would have to get past the gate, and the gate was guarded.

I decided to test it. Not all guards loved their job, or were good at it. Some just sat and smoked. Some slept.

I moved in closer, wandering instead of walking so I wouldn't draw the attention of the guards. I wandered by like I was invisible.

I sat down on the wide steps a short distance from the gate to see what kind of guards they were.

A small group of women wearing high-heeled shoes, nice saris and lots of jewelry approached the opening in the fence. They were talking and laughing.

The guards stopped them.

"Show us your bags."

The women were all carrying large purses.

"We need to examine your bags."

The women began to argue. "You're not looking in our purses. Why would we let you do that?"

"I am sorry, madam. We must look inside."

"Look inside for what? Do you think we are terrorists? Do you think we are carrying bombs?"

The women kept arguing and the guards kept insisting.

Finally, with a lot of foot-stomping and threatening to get the guards fired, the women allowed their purses to be searched. They huddled around the guards while their bags were opened.

I jumped into action.

I climbed the steps and slid in through the gate behind the backs of the women. No one noticed me.

The mall went on and on. It was very different from the markets, where everything was crowded together. The markets were alive. Merchants sold chickens that squawked and vegetables picked from the fields outside Kolkata and brought in on the early trains. Markets smelled like flowers and dung cakes, pakoras frying and cilantro being chopped. They were noisy and hot, and when it rained, they were a real mess.

The mall had wide corridors that got swept a lot. There was no garbage on the floor. The air was cool and clean. There were no live animals, just displays of jewelry, clothes and dishes behind glass. There were no smells other than the perfume worn by all the shopping ladies.

The meals were all served in one area. The garbage bins were out back, but I was hoping for food that hadn't made it into the garbage yet.

I climbed some stairs and came out into a large room filled with light and tables and music. This room was surrounded by little cooking places. People went up to a stall and got pizza or sandwiches or Chinese food or vegetarian food. I heard ice chink into big plastic cups and I heard Coke and fizzy orange drinks land on top of the ice.

I sat at the back behind a plastic plant and kept my eyes open. There were guards here, too, and workers who would swoop down on the tables and take away the leftovers the second the customers got up to leave.

A family sat nearby having lunch.

"Finish your pizza," the father said.

"I don't want it," the little boy whined. "I want a hotdog."

"You said you wanted pizza."

"Hotdog."

"I don't like the look of the hotdogs," the mother said. "You like pizza. Eat your pizza."

"No."

"And drink your Coke. We don't waste."

They kept arguing. When they weren't telling their child to eat, the parents argued about other things.

"We go to your brother's house every week. Is it too much to ask that we skip one week?"

"All I do for you. Why can't you do this for me?"

It hurt my head. I wanted to move, but I wanted their food more.

I tried my special magic to make things happen.

Leave the table, I told them silently. Leave the table and leave the food.

It wasn't working. On and on they sat.

I tried to remember the last time I had eaten, not counting the unripe melon I threw up.

It was the day before yesterday, I decided. I had begged some rupees from the tourists on Sudder Street.

"You should be in school," they had said. Then they argued about whether or not they should give me money.

"It only encourages them," one tourist said. "We should give it to a charity."

"We should go shopping," another said. "When the economy is strong, everybody wins."

They talked and I stood in front of them with my hand open, wanting to snatch the five-rupee note out of the tourist's hand so I wouldn't have to listen to them anymore. But tourists don't like it when you take money from them. I watched another child do that once. They held onto him and called the police on their cellphone. He always begged in front of the Indian museum, but I never saw him again after that.

Leave the table, I tried again. Leave the food.

"I want ice cream!"

"Why can't you make him behave? Every time we go out, he acts up. Finish your Coke."

"Maybe if you were home more instead of always off with those friends of yours."

"Let's just go. You don't want your pizza? Leave it."

"Ice cream!"

"You're not getting ice cream. I'm not buying you another thing."

The child screeched and wailed, but the family got up. Customers' eyes followed the wailing as they left the eating area.

I moved fast.

With one hand I folded the pizza and stuck it in my pocket with the nail polish. With my other hand I stuffed my mouth with curried potatoes, dal, tomato chutney and the little bit of cucumber salad the mother had left. I grabbed the pieces of paratha and downed the rest of the cold Coke in one gulp. Then I ran before the guards could grab me.

The Coke bubbles rose up in my stomach. Out came a huge burp. I thought it was funny. I didn't care if the other diners did not.

I ate the paratha as I walked through the mall. Food in my stomach made all the difference. I could look and enjoy and pass the time in clean, cool air.

"Only four more shopping days to Christmas," a young man called out. He stood outside a shoe store trying to encourage people to come in and buy.

I kept wandering and trying to distract myself from eating the pizza in my pocket. I was still hungry, but I would be more hungry later.

I stopped in front of a bookstore. There was a poster in the window of a human body cut in two. One half showed the bones. The other half showed the organs. It was like the picture Dr. Indra showed me in the hospital.

I put my finger against the glass, over the picture of the human heart. I put my other hand over my own heart.

I could feel it beating. I remembered what it sounded like through the stethoscope.

Out of the heart came red lines that traveled all over the body, including to the spot on my arm where Dr. Indra had taken out my beautiful blood.

So, blood came out of the heart. Was it made there? Where did it go?

I stared hard at the poster, trying to figure it out.

"Get away from there!"

The bookstore security guard tried to shoo me away.

"Get away!" he said. "This has nothing to do with you!"

"I look like that inside," I told him. "So do you."

"Do you have money? You have no money. This is not for you."

"I have plenty of money," I said, patting my pocket where the folded-up pizza was. "And I'd like to buy …" I reached into my memory for the right words. "I'd like to buy a biology book."

I walked past the guard into the store.

I didn't get far.

"Get out," the manager said. "Take your filthy hands off the books and get out. There is nothing here for you." To the guard he said, "If you let this happen again, you're fired."

The guard tried to grab me, but I left on my own.

I was mad. How did they know I didn't have any money? Could they see into my pocket? Maybe I had as much money as those fancy ladies who didn't want their purses searched.

And then I saw my reflection in one of the windows.

I had been looking at the inside of the windows, so I hadn't noticed it before.

Now I saw it.

I was filthy. I had stayed away from the river because I was afraid I might run into Dr. Indra there. My kurta was torn and covered in grime. My hair was knotted and matted. I scratched my head a lot because ants crawled around in it at night and that made it all bunch up. Wind and living did the rest.

They were right, I thought. Books were not for me. I probably didn't even look like everybody else inside. Under my skin, there was probably just more dirt.

I left the mall.

I walked out past the guards at the gate, who

yelled, "How did you get in here? Get out!" I tried to sit on the steps, but they chased me away.

I sat on the curb across the street. They couldn't stop me from doing that.

But it didn't make me feel any better.

11

Feet

AND THEN I FORCED myself to do what I had avoided doing since I'd left the hospital.

I looked at my feet.

Even caked with dirt, I could see they were a mess.

There were large nasty-looking sores on the sides and the bottoms. There were blisters from the burns that were green and puffy. There were cuts from glass and bruises and scrapes from all the falls I'd had just that morning, hitching rides on the backs of trucks.

And they smelled bad.

Not just ordinary street-dirt bad. Worse. Like walking-by-a-dog-that-had-been-dead-for-three-days bad.

I looked at the feet of the people passing by. I was close to the ground, in a good position to look at feet. I saw feet in high heels, feet in army boots, feet that were bare and feet in canvas runners. I saw the dancing feet of children who were eager to get into the mall and the tired feet of tradespeople pushing their barrows.

What was the worst that could happen? My feet wouldn't fall off. So what if they had sores? So what if they smelled bad? Nobody ever died from having bad-smelling feet.

Or did they? I didn't know.

"I don't know anything," I said out loud.

Maybe I should try to make my way back to Jharia. I could pick up coal, live with the woman who was not my aunt and it wouldn't matter that I didn't know how the body made blood or what it took to make someone die. I knew how to find bits of coal on the ground, pick them up and put them in a bag. A lot of people lived their whole lives that way.

"Get along. Keep moving."

I thought the guard was snarling at me. I wasn't sure I had the strength to argue with him, even though he was a mall guard and had no power over who sat on the curb. Of course, that wouldn't stop him from hitting me anyway if he wanted to.

"Spare a rupee for my baby?"

The voice was weak, but there was a lull in the traffic and I heard her.

I looked up.

A thin woman in a torn and dirty sari was slowly climbing the stairs to the gate where the guards stood.

Her baby was in a pouch across her shoulder. She cradled it with one arm and held the other arm out, the palm of her hand open to the sun.

"Please, one rupee."

She would never get anything. After months on the streets, I could generally tell who was not worth begging from. Guards didn't get to be guards by doing anyone any favors.

"Get away from here!"

The woman kept climbing.

Mall customers pushed by her. They ignored her open hand and hurried through the security check to get into the stores.

Four more shopping days to Christmas, I thought. Four days suddenly seemed like a long time.

I realized that I had gotten through these months by not thinking about time. I thought about food, and somewhere to sleep, and being entertained, but I never thought about time.

What was there to think about? Each day would be the same. Some days I would eat more, some days I would eat less. Some nights I would sleep in a cemetery. Some nights I would spend on the pavement. Sometimes I washed in the river. Usually I didn't wash at all.

Just like on the best day of my life when I stood on the edge of the coal pit and looked into my future, I looked into my future now.

I could see it.

My future was the woman with the baby, who was walking with her head down across the road to my curb, her palm still open and hanging down empty at her side.

She got closer to me. She was crying. A thin wail rose up from the pouch across her chest.

"It's a lousy day," I said to her.

"It's just ..." She eased herself down onto the curb. Then she said, "It's just an ordinary day."

I reached into my pocket and took out the folded-up piece of pizza. There was some pocket fuzz on the crust. I brushed it off.

"Here," I said.

She took the pizza from me and stared at it for a moment, as if she wasn't quite sure what it was. Then she took a small bite of the crust, softened it with her mouth and took it out and gave it to her baby. I saw two tiny hands come out of the pouch to grab hold of the food. The wailing stopped.

The woman looked up at me.

"Thank you," she said.

I walked away.

I kept walking. I had a long way to go.

The mall was in the Salt Lake area of Kolkata, far from the middle part of the city. I could have hopped rides to get back downtown. But walking seemed like the right thing to do.

I didn't know what was going to happen to me. I couldn't picture it. I walked through the streets as if it were my last walk.

I walked past the smooth green lawns and marble palaces of the neighborhoods where rich people lived. I walked along the narrow pathways between the small square lakes where fish were hatched and caught. I walked through the bamboo bustees and pavement dwellers, past shops and mosques, movie theaters and yoga parks with their pergolas and quiet gardens. I walked as the sun went down and the headlights shone on the thick dust and exhaust that turned the air to fog.

I grew very tired.

But I kept on walking.

I was afraid that if I stopped, I would think. And if I thought about it, I would talk myself out of it.

It was quite late at night by the time I got to Dr. Indra's hospital. The gates across the driveway were closed and locked shut.

Across the street was a row of large cement construction pipes. I climbed into one.

From pipes on either side of me came the sounds of snoring. Others had the same idea I did. But I didn't sleep.

I kept my eyes on the gates. I waited out the night and tried hard not to think.

At dawn the guards came out to open the gates. I jumped up.

I walked quickly across the road and into the hospital. Up the stairs, and then I was back in the room full of beds and monsters.

Everyone was still asleep. They were just lumps under sheets. Just lumps. They did not look like monsters.

I remembered which bed I had been in. It was the one next to the one next to the window. I walked right over to it and stood at the end.

Someone was sleeping there.

I assumed it was a woman because everyone else in the room was a woman. I couldn't tell for sure because of all the bandages over the face. There were bandages on the arms and across the chest.

I had walked a very long way and sat up all night in order to be back in the hospital, and now I didn't know what to do. It had never occurred to me that there might not be room for me.

I had no other plans.

And so I did the only thing I could think of to do.

I banged on the bedframe.

"Get up," I said loudly. "You're sleeping in my bed."

12

A Decision

NOT EVERYONE WAS GLAD to see me.

In fact, for several hours, until Dr. Indra came, nobody was glad.

The women in the ward were not glad. I had woken them up from a sound sleep, ages before the tea was hot and at the hour of the morning when mosquitoes were most hungry. It was hard to get back to sleep with the noise of their buzzing.

The nurses were not glad. They had been awake and working all night. Their shifts were coming to an end and they were busy writing notes and shuffling papers around. None of them had been on duty when I had been in the hospital before. They didn't know me. They didn't know that was my bed.

And the security guards were not happy. I hadn't climbed the fence or broken any windows. I had waited until the gate was unlocked. But I caused a commotion, and they were tired, too.

"If she can get in, anybody can get in," I heard.

"No one is coming in," someone else said. "People run away from us. They don't sneak into places to be with us."

"And yet here she is," the first voice said. "I knew she was trouble."

"Miss, please come with us to the waiting room." A guard stood beside me. I waited for him to hit me, but he must have been too tired. "The doctors will be in soon."

I knew I couldn't leave that room. If I did, I might leave the hospital, and I needed to be there. But I was scared. I held onto the metal frame of that bed and I did not move. I kept my eyes on my hands.

"Dr. Indra wants me to be here," I said. "This is my bed."

They left me alone.

The guard went away and the nurses worked around me. They changed bandages, carried bed-pans, fluffed pillows and gave out pills. Sometimes they said "Excuse me," but they didn't sound angry. And nobody hit me.

I had walked a long way and sat up all night. Once the excitement of my arrival died down, the ward got quiet again. The walk and the night started to catch up with me. My eyes wanted to shut and my body wanted to slide to the floor.

"You can sit." A patient with a cane pushed a chair over to the end of the bed. "No one will think less of you if you do."

She left the chair beside me. I tried to ignore it, but it called to me. My knees bent. I sat down, and in moments I was sound asleep with my head on the bed.

"GOOD MORNING, Valli."

Dr. Indra had arrived.

"Would you like to stop drooling on Laxmi and tell me why you are here?"

I shook my head clear of sleep and stood up.

"My bandages fell off."

"You came here to get new bandages put on your feet?"

"Yes."

"Anything else?"

I want to be you, I wanted to say, but I couldn't.

"Just the bandages," I said. I hoped she would be able to guess that I wanted more.

Instead she shook her head and said, "Come with me."

She led me out into the hall and sat down with me on a bench.

"If all you want me to do is bandage your feet, then I'm afraid I can't help you."

"You won't help me?"

"That would not be helping you. It would be hurting you."

"No, it wouldn't."

"Yes. You would go back out into the street and continue living your life, all the while doing more damage to your feet and to the rest of your nerves. I am a doctor. I took an oath to do no harm. Simply giving you bandages and letting you leave would be doing you harm. I would be going against my oath."

"What's an oath?"

"It's a solemn promise."

"To who?"

"To myself. And it's very important to keep the promises we make to ourselves. So, if all you want is a bandage, I can't help you."

I hung my head and looked at my hands.

"What should I want?" I asked.

"You should want to get well. Leprosy is curable if you take the pills. Your wounds are treatable if you allow us to treat them. You are a child. As far as we know, you have no parents or guardian. I could arrange things to make myself responsible for you and force you to take treatments. But I want you to make the decision."

"What would I have to do?"

"You would have to stay here for a while. We will test you to see what kind of drugs you need. Some people need only one pill. Others need up to three different kinds of pills. You would have to take this medicine every day for six months to two years, depending on the test results. And you would have to let us treat your wounds properly, which might mean surgery."

I didn't understand the word surgery, but I had other worries.

"I would have to stay here all the time?"

"Yes. For a while. Then we'll see."

"But I could go out during the day and come back here to sleep."

"No," Dr. Indra said. "Staying here means staying here. Not running off into the street whenever you feel like it or whenever you get scared. Living here."

"I can't," I told her.

"Tell me why not."

"How will I eat?"

She smiled. "We have food here. We fed you before. Don't you remember?"

Why couldn't she understand? I leaned in close to her and whispered, "I don't have any money."

Dr. Indra laughed. "I didn't think you did! All over the world, people send us money so that you can get treated."

"Me?"

"And others like you. But it's not a gift. They expect something for their money."

"What? I don't have anything."

Then I remembered my talk with the old man and his pet goat. I had quite a lot, really.

"They expect you to get healthy and go on to do great things with your life." Dr. Indra stood up. "I have to start my shift. Sit here as long as you need to. Let me know when you have made your decision."

She walked away, then turned back again.

"One more thing," she said. "There will be no more talk of monsters. You will treat these people with respect. You have the same disease they do."

"Will I end up like them?" I pushed in my nose and clawed up my hands.

"No," the doctor said, walking away again.

"How do you know?" I called after her.

"Because," she called back, "you have me!"

I stood at the top of the stairs and watched her walk down. I went back to the bench and stayed there.

There really was nothing to think about. Free food, a free place to sleep on a mat that was even softer than the grassy graves in the Englishmen's cemetery. My feet would get fixed and maybe Dr. Indra would let me look through the microscope again.

"Tea?"

I looked up. A woman with part of her nose gone was pushing a cart full of cups and tea pots. She was hard to look at.

"Are you a patient?" I asked.

"I used to be," she said. "Now I work here. I'm the tea lady."

She poured me some tea with a hand that had some of its fingers worn away. She held out the cup for me to take.

I stared at it. She put the tea down on the bench beside me and rolled the cart away.

I couldn't make myself pick up the cup.

Maybe I couldn't do this, I thought, as I watched the steam rise up from the tea.

The tea lady pushed her cart over to the nurses' office. I could see through the large window that several nurses were leaning over files and charts, writing and talking. They said, "Good morning" and "Thank you" to the tea lady as she poured them their morning cups, then pushed the cart into the next ward.

The nurses drank from the cups, talked and wrote. To them it was just another ordinary day.

I picked up my own cup and drank the tea.

It tasted good. It tasted like tea.

And then I went in search of Dr. Indra. I was ready to tell her my decision.

13

Clean

"THIS WILL BE your bed."

I was back in the same ward, close to the same bed. My old bed was still occupied by the woman with all the bandages. They were putting me in the bed right next to her.

"You're close to the window," Dr. Indra said. "You can keep an eye on the world."

"Are you going to do that to me?" I pointed to the woman in the bandages.

"If you give me any trouble, I might." But she said it with a smile, so she was probably joking.

I started to sit on the bed but she stopped me.

"You're filthy."

"Do you want me to go down to the river to wash?"

She had something else in mind.

The tea lady, whose name was Usha, did more than just pour tea.

"The washing room is through here," she said. "Let's get you clean."

At the end of the ward was a small lavatory with showers.

"I can do this myself," I said.

It was just the two of us in the washroom. Usha stood between me and the door.

"Dr. Indra asked me to help you."

"I can do it," I said again.

She stepped toward me to help me take off my kurta.

I stepped back.

"Valli, look at me."

I raised my eyes to her face, then looked down again.

"Don't look away," she said. "Look as long and as hard as you need to. Look at me until you see me."

She held up her hands so I could look at them, too, the fingers only half of what they should have been.

I did as she asked.

I looked. Hard.

And something happened.

I stopped seeing the caved-in nose. I stopped seeing the damaged eye with its drooping eyelid and milky-looking eyeball. And I stopped seeing the stubs of fingers.

Instead I saw the face of the woman who had brought me a good cup of tea. I saw little lines around the corners of her eyes. I saw kindness in her smile. I saw a woman who was stubborn and hard working and did not want to hurt me.

"I see you," I said.

She smiled. And then she scrubbed.

Usha didn't have all her fingers, but what she had left were strong. She rubbed and scrubbed even harder than the women at Mrs. Mukerjee's. I kept saying, "Owww!" and all she said was, "Oh, does that hurt?" and she kept scrubbing.

She handed me a hospital gown and had me stand in front of a mirror while she combed out my hair.

I hadn't had many chances to look at myself in my life. The woman who was not my aunt had no mirror in her house. Well, she had a small one once, but the man who was not my uncle broke it when he was drinking.

I had looked at my reflection in shop windows, and a furniture store on Park Street had mirror squares stuck to the outside of it. In the early mornings the shop front would be crowded with women and men who lived on the pavement and were checking their hair before going off to work.

But a whole big mirror like this? Never.

I took a good long look at my face. I liked what I saw. If I tilted it a certain way and let one side be partly in shadow, I looked a little like the movie-star women whose pictures were on posters and billboards.

Then I covered up part of my nose and pretended it had been taken by leprosy, like Usha's.

I still looked good, I decided.

Then I backed up and started to do a Bollywood dance that I had learned in Jharia. I watched myself sway and twist.

Again, I looked good.

"Hold still," Usha said, but she wasn't angry. "No lice. Good for you." She put a part down the middle of my head and wound my hair into two long braids that hung down my back. "Maybe we can find some ribbons for your braids."

It felt funny walking back into the ward in a gown with no trousers. But I liked the feel of the braids bouncing against my shoulders.

"Here she is," Usha announced to the other women. "All clean and fresh. Everyone, this is Valli."

I really looked at the other patients for the first time. Some looked normal, like any other women, and had just small bandages on their hands or feet. Others had feet propped up in big casts and bandages on their faces. Some were sitting up and reading. Others were resting.

They all smiled and said hello.

Except one.

"Is she going to wake us up rudely every morning like she did today?" she asked.

"As I recall, Mrs. Das, you brought no peace to us in your early days here." The woman in the bed beside mine put her hand over her cellphone to talk to the grumpy-looking woman who didn't like me. She then went back to her phone conversation. File folders and notebooks were open all over the top of her bed, and she kept looking at them as she talked.

I sat on the edge of my bed. The last time I had been too sleepy and too scared to notice much. Now I wanted to notice everything.

In the home of the woman who was not my aunt, I had slept on the floor. Everyone did. That was all there was. In the streets I slept on sidewalks and benches, parks, graves and beaches.

This was the first time I would have a bed.

"Do I have to share this with anyone?" I whispered.

"It's all yours," came a voice.

The woman in the bandages could talk.

I swung my feet off the edge of the bed. It was fun.

"Can you swing your feet?" I asked the bandages.

"Maybe soon," she replied. "My legs aren't too bad."

"I'm Valli," I said.

"I'm Laxmi."

"Do you have leprosy, too? You must have it bad."

"I was burned," she said.

"It was one of those kitchen accidents." The woman with the cellphone was finished with her phone conversation. "Her husband's family wanted more dowry. When there wasn't any more, someone poured kerosene on her and set her on fire. I don't know how she's still alive. And I don't know how she stands the pain. At fifteen!"

I looked at Laxmi. I thought of Elamma. I thought of the man who was not my uncle. It made me want to go back to Jharia and get her.

The cellphone rang again, and she started another call.

Some of the patients propped up their pillows at the back of the beds. They leaned against them when they sat up.

I did the same. It was comfortable.

I looked around the ward. Everyone was ignoring me. Some were dozing. Laxmi's eyes were closed. The grumpy woman was scowling at me. I ran my hands over my new braids, breathed in the clean smell of my skin and clothes and waited to see what would happen next.

"YOU'RE GOING TO NEED a skin graft."

The doctor — another doctor, a man — was looking closely at my feet, along with Dr. Indra.

"You will need to explain that to her, Dr. Siva," Dr. Indra said. "This is a girl who needs explanations."

Dr. Siva took a small mirror out of the pocket of his white jacket. He set it up so that I could see the bottoms of my feet more easily.

I squished up my face with disgust. My feet had looked terrible when they were covered with dirt. All cleaned up, they looked even worse. Large deep sores looked like they had been carved out of my feet with a knife.

"They don't hurt," I said.

"That's the leprosy germ at work," Dr. Siva said. "It eats away at your nerves. The job of nerves is to make us feel things, especially pain. It's a very important job because if we don't feel pain, we don't know that we're hurting ourselves."

"Dr. Indra said you can't fix nerves."

"Not yet," he said. "Maybe one day. But we can stop the damage from getting worse. You're going to start taking the drugs today. And I can repair these holes in your feet by taking some skin from another part of your body and patching it over the wounds."

"You'll take some skin?"

"Probably from your upper leg."

I rubbed my thigh. I was trying to figure it out.

"You mean you'll cut it out? That will hurt!"

"You won't feel a thing," Dr. Indra said. "We'll put you to sleep."

"I'll wake up!"

"They did the same thing to me," the cellphone woman said. "I'm healing beautifully. Isn't that right, doctors?"

She had bandages on her feet.

"I want to see," I said.

"Neeta is an expert," Dr. Indra said as she undid one of the bandages on the cellphone woman's feet.

I looked at the big wound on Neeta's foot. It was covered over by a round patch of skin.

"That does not look good," I said.

"It will," said Dr. Siva. "And so will your feet, I promise you. Ask us any questions you want. At any time." He turned to Dr. Indra. "When do you suggest we do it?"

"I'd like to wait until the middle of January. She's quite malnourished. Let's build her up a bit."

"The middle of January it is."

He went on to the next patient.

Dr. Indra started to bandage my feet.

"I know I can't keep you on the bed all the time, but please, as a favor to me, stay off your feet as much as possible. Don't make your injuries worse. Look out the window, talk to your neighbors, and help us make you well and strong."

My feet were dressed again in bright white bandages. Dr. Indra gave me cloth slippers to wear over them when I walked around.

"Dr. Indra?"

"What is it, Valli?"

"The people who are paying for this. Do they really expect me to do something great with my life?"

"They really do. And you know what?"

"What?"

"So do I."

14

A New Type of Roti

THE PILL WAS SMALL, yellow and round. I tossed it to the back of my throat the way the nurse said to do, and gulped it down with a big glass of cold water.

"That's it?" I asked her.

"That's it," she said. "One each day for a year. When you take it, think about it eating the germs that are eating away at your nerves."

The nurse poured water for Laxmi and held a straw to her lips so she could drink through her bandages.

"Where does blood go?" I asked her.

"What do you mean?"

"It gets made in the heart, right? And goes all through your body on those red lines? Where does it go when it gets to the end of the lines?"

"Those red lines are called veins and arteries. And your blood doesn't go away. It keeps moving through your body. But you are right. The heart pumps it."

"Like Sealdah," I said. "The heart is like a train station. Trains aren't made there, but they come and they go."

The nurse looked at me with a funny expression on her face.

"You're going to be a scientist some day," she said.

"Is Dr. Indra a scientist?"

The nurse smiled. "We all are."

She moved on. I thought about my heart as a train station. I put my hand on my chest where the stethoscope had gone, and I felt it thumping.

"Try your wrists, too," Neeta suggested. She held up her own wrist and showed me where to put my fingers. It took some time, but I found the spot.

"It works on both wrists!" I explained.

"On your neck, too." Neeta put her fingers on the side of her throat. "It's called a pulse."

I found my own pulse on my neck. Then I had to see if I could find it on someone else. Laxmi was the closest. I could reach one of her wrists without getting off my bed.

I found her pulse. Then I put on my slippers and moved on to the other patients.

Most of the women didn't mind. The grouchy woman, Mrs. Das, tucked her wrists into her armpits when I came close, so I didn't even ask.

Maybe she doesn't have a pulse, I thought.

I got so involved in finding everyone's pulse that I often forgot to notice whether the wrist I was holding had a hand with fingers on it or not. Once, when I did notice that the fingers had been eaten away, I was so excited about feeling the blood beating through the veins that I didn't care about the fingers.

The lunch cart came around. I tucked into the rice and dal that people around the world had paid for. I imagined people from all over the place getting together and discussing what I would like to eat. I licked my plate clean. I didn't want to waste a single grain of rice.

For the next three days I slept and ate. I found everyone's pulses again, except for Mrs. Das. I could have tried for the pulse in her throat, but she was in such a bad mood that I was afraid she might bite me. Dr. Indra let me listen to my heart through her stethoscope again. I took my pill every day with a big glass of water, and I tried to stay off my feet.

That was easier than I thought it would be. I was very, very tired. It was as though I had been saving up my tiredness all my life in order to feel it now.

"I'm the same way," Neeta said when I woke up from my morning nap just in time to eat lunch. "Most of us here are. The only time we can rest is when we're in the hospital."

I saw women nodding all over the ward.

"Tired from what?" I asked. The only other people I knew with leprosy spent their time dodging stones beside the railway tracks.

And the fortune teller, I reminded himself. And maybe there were others I didn't know about.

"I'm a sales director for a health-supplies company," Neeta said. "I have fourteen salespeople working under me, nine of them men. Although, if one of them doesn't change his attitude by the time I get out of here, there will be eight men instead of nine."

"Don't you have leprosy?" I asked.

"Oh, yes," she said. "Or I did. But I took the pills and now I'm cured. But my nerves are damaged and I developed bad ulcers on my feet."

"Ulcers?"

"Sores. It's my job to check up on all the men who work for me. I was running around fixing their mistakes, and I didn't take proper care of my feet. So I came here to get fixed up. But even here," she held up her phone, "they call me with their problems."

I wanted to see her phone. I had never held one before. I wanted to see what was in the folders and notebooks on her bed. I wanted her to explain everything to me.

But instead, as soon as my lunch was finished, I fell back asleep.

I woke up the next morning feeling like I had finally caught up with my tiredness.

"I've got my energy back," I announced.

"Wonderful," said Mrs. Das, although her face didn't look as though she thought it was wonderful.

I couldn't stay in bed.

I fetched the broom from the corner of the ward and swept under everyone's bed. I went out into the hallway and looked in the doors of the other wards. I had a great time saying "Good morning" and making the namaste to everyone until a nurse shooed me back to my own ward.

I kept busy there for a little bit, with breakfast and another washing, but after that I ran out of things to do. I thought of checking everyone's pulse, but a lot of the patients were sleeping again. I already knew they didn't like it when I woke them up.

I played little finger games with Laxmi for a few minutes. I tapped her finger, then she tapped mine, and we kept up a rhythm that way while I sang — quietly — one of the songs I'd learned in Jharia. But she couldn't do anything for very long. She was only awake for a little while at a time.

"They have her on heavy drugs for the pain," Neeta said. She was reading through her folders again.

I took that as an invitation.

"What are you doing?" I moved in for a closer look.

"I'm charting sales figures for each area of my district," she said. "If a certain product sells better in one neighborhood than in another, I want to know why. Is it the salesperson? Is it the soap? But I can't know why until I know what's going on. Can you read? Do you know about numbers?"

"I can read a little, in both Hindi and English," I said proudly. "And I can count to one hundred."

"Then you'll be able to understand this. It's not hard. Look."

She showed me a circle divided by lines.

"This is called a pie chart."

"Pie?"

"For you it's called a roti chart. The circle represents all the sales of our company's products for three months in one area by one salesperson. Do you understand?"

At first I wasn't sure about the word represents. But then I nodded. It was like a train station representing a heart.

She went on. "Each section represents one of our products." She went around the circle. "Hair cream, hand soap, shampoo, shaving lotion and so on. I look at this chart and see that in this area, we have sold more shaving lotion than shampoo. That's different from what I see on other charts, where shampoo is the bigger seller. Now I think about why. The sales rep for the area is a man. Is he selling only to other men? Is he too pushy around women so they don't want to buy from him? Is he too shy around women and doesn't approach them at all? Or is it something else entirely? From this information," she tapped the chart, "I can figure out which questions to ask to solve the problem."

"Where do you live?" I asked her.

"In Howrah, the other side of the river."

"In the garbage piles beside the railway tracks?"

She laughed. "Oh, no! I have a very nice apartment in a new building. Railway tracks? Where did you get such an idea?"

Then she gave me some paper and a pencil and showed me how to make my own roti chart.

"There are ten patients in this ward," she said. "Divide the circle into ten equal sections. Equal means all the same size."

I went back to my bed to do that. It took several tries, but I did it.

"Now find out how many of the patients have leprosy and how many have burns."

I went from bed to bed. Everyone told me what they had except for Mrs. Das.

"She has leprosy," Neeta said. "It has affected her sense of humor. What are your results?"

"Seven have leprosy, three have burns."

"Show that on your chart," she said, but she didn't tell me how to do it.

I went back to my bed and thought about it. When I figured it out, I knew without asking Neeta that I was absolutely right. Absolutely.

After that I did roti charts on how many took sugar, or milk, or sugar and milk, with their morning tea. I charted whether they were married or not and who preferred rice to roti.

I fell asleep late in the afternoon with my bed sprinkled with my lovely charts.

The nurse woke me up to take my pill. She gathered the charts into a tidy stack, put them in a spare cardboard folder she had in her office and tucked it all under the corner of my pillow. I swallowed my pill with a big glass of water, put my head back down on my pillow and stretched my arm out across the folder.

I fell back into a sound, restful sleep.

15

Midnight Clear

"VALLI? VALLI, wake up."

I opened my eyes. Dr. Indra was sitting on my bed. It was night time. I'd slept through dinner.

I sat up. "I'm hungry."

Dr. Indra laughed. "Of course you are. We'll get you some food in a minute. But first I have something for you. Do you know what tomorrow is?"

I shook my head.

"Tomorrow is Christmas Day."

"No more shopping days left."

"No more. Tomorrow there will be a Christmas party here. You'll have a very special dinner and everyone will get presents. But I won't be here. I'm spending Christmas with my parents. So I have something I wanted to give you tonight."

She reached behind her back and brought out a

package wrapped in pretty paper. Santa Claus was smiling, over and over. No one was beating him up.

She handed it to me.

I held it in my hands. It was heavy. I wasn't sure what I was supposed to do with it.

"It's a present," she said. "You have to take the paper off to see what's inside."

I found the ends of the paper. They were stuck down with tape. I carefully loosened it all so the paper wouldn't tear.

"What is it?" asked Laxmi.

"Yes," said Neeta. "Show us."

It was a book. I tried to sound out the title, but the words were too big for me.

"Biology of the Human Body," Dr. Indra read for me. "This is my old biology book from school. A lot of it will be too hard for you now, but you'll be able to understand some of it."

"She'll understand all of it before long," Neeta said. "She's a smart one. We'll probably both be working for her one day."

I opened it up.

Some pages had tea stains. Most pages had handwritten notes scribbled in pen in the margins and lines underneath some sentences.

In the middle of the book were pages made out of clear plastic. They had drawings of the human body on them that could be flipped back to show the bones, then the organs, then even more organs. And almost every paper page had pictures on it.

"Why are you giving me this?"

"This book is yours to keep," Dr. Indra said. "You don't have to do anything for it. That's what a present is. It's giving something and not wanting anything back. I'm giving it to you because I like you."

Like the pizza I gave the woman at the mall, I thought. And the blanket from the Metropole Hotel. And the soap I gave away. And all the other things I had borrowed in Kolkata, then passed along to someone else.

"I'll just borrow it," I said. "And when I know everything in it, I'll pass it to someone else who needs to know."

"Then pass this along, too. Let me give you a hug." Dr. Indra reached out and put her arms around me.

I wasn't sure what she was doing. I wasn't afraid, because I knew she wouldn't hurt me, but the hug was strange. I had never had one before. I could feel our hearts beating together.

"Merry Christmas, Valli," she said, and then she left.

Bells started to ring.

All the women who were able to get out of bed gathered around the window. They pulled open the inside glass and pushed out the shutters so the sound could come through clearly.

I joined them there.

From all over Kolkata, I heard the sounds of bells.

"It's Christmas," someone said. "It's midnight. Merry Christmas, everyone!"

Usha pushed her trolley into the ward.

"Who would like a special treat to celebrate the holiday?"

"Is that ice cream?" Mrs. Das asked. "I haven't had ice cream since I was a child."

"Maybe that's what's wrong with her," Neeta mumbled. "Come on, Valli. Mrs. Das may be greedy as well as grumpy. We don't want her eating our share."

But I stayed at the window, looking out into the night.

I knew there were people out there who were not getting ice cream that night. They were sleeping where I had slept. They were cold, or scared, or hungry or sick.

I thought again of the woman who was not my aunt, and wondered if she or her children had ever tasted ice cream.

Maybe, one day, I could take them some.

"Why am I so lucky?" I asked the night.

"Valli, are you all right?" Usha came to stand beside me.

"Dr. Indra gave me a hug," I said. "I'm supposed to pass it on. Can I pass it on to you?"

And then I was hugging her. And it felt just as good as hugging the doctor.

One of the patients held out the last dish of ice cream.

"Hurry up, Valli," she said. "We're waiting for you."

I had friends, I thought. And they were waiting for me. How about that? The fortune teller was right.

I went to get my ice cream.

I could hardly wait to see what would happen to me next.

Author's Note

LEPROSY IS CAUSED by a bacterium that destroys the nerves in the cooler parts of the human body, especially in the hands, feet, skin and eyes. It can begin to show itself as white or discolored patches on the skin. If it remains untreated, it starts to take feeling out of hands and feet. People become unable to feel pain, and they can't tell when they become injured. Their injuries lead to infection and permanent damage.

Leprosy is one of the oldest recorded diseases in human history. Because of its ability to disfigure, it is a disease that has been much feared and misunderstood. In many communities, people with leprosy are still cast out of mainstream society because the community doesn't understand that leprosy is hard to get and can be cured.

The world is making progress. Real efforts are being made so people can be diagnosed, treated and restart their lives with the proper supports so that they don't become injured again. But there is still a long way to go.

Leprosy is primarily a disease of poverty, spread by close contact in countries where large numbers of people live together in small rooms or houses. People living in poverty work much harder than people with financial security, and they don't have the ability to take time off to heal, so they often become reinjured. Folks with disabilities in poor countries have few resources, and the country's infrastructure is not set up to help them. Add the stigma of leprosy to that disability, and daily life can become very difficult.

Still, the world is getting closer and closer to wiping out leprosy. The generation of young people who are reading this book may well be the ones to finally make leprosy history.

The royalties from this book are being donated to:

The Leprosy Mission of Canada
100 Mural Street, Suite 100
Richmond Hill, Ontario L4B 1J3
905-886-2887 www.leprosy.ca info@leprosy.ca

Glossary

bhaji – Vegetable fritter.

Bollywood – Indian film industry, based in Mumbai, which used to be called Bombay.

buffalo – Water buffalo, common in Asia.

bullock – A male buffalo; also used as an insult.

bustee – A neighborhood of makeshift houses for people living in poverty.

channa – Chickpeas.

cheroot – Small hand-rolled cigar.

dal – Porridge made from lentils, peas or chickpeas.

desi-daru – Homemade liquor.

dosa – A type of pancake.

dupatta – A long scarf.

Durga-puja – A Hindu religious festival.

ghat – Steps leading down to water.

Hindi – One of India's official languages.

Kali – A Hindu goddess.

Kolkata – The capital city in West Bengal, India; used to be called Calcutta.

kurta – A long, loose shirt.

lungi – A garment that wraps around the waist; worn by men.